Wretchedness

Andrzej Tichý

Translated by Nichola Smalley

PRAISE FOR

WRETCHEDNESS

'What can a survivor do with their history? Can you be loyal
to the friends you left behind? Andrzej Tichý turns this
wretched reality into something poignant. His polyphonic
novel has a rough, rhythmic melody and a ferocious rage.'

August Prize Judges

'Post-political, that's what I want to call Andrzej
Tichý's arrestingly acute writing. [. . .] A terrifying
and hard story that doesn't forget to occasionally
burst out into something gripping and beautiful.'

Jonas Thente, *Dagens Nyheter*

'Tichý writes a delirious, detailed prose, studded with
Malmö slang and contemporary verve. The language
pours forth over the pages like a contaminated river,
full of filth, despair and anxiety, an associative flow
of long, disjointed, almost endless sentences.'

Eva Johansson, *Svenska Dagbladet*

'In virtuosically rendered language; full of the poetry of
spoken word, the innovation of contemporary slang, and
the philosophical verve of great literature, Tichý gives a
voice to the lost "brothers" of his youth. To follow this
frantic, mournful, bamboozling, pleading, smart, childish,
would-be hard, bragging, desperate and despairing collective
memory is to "hear" a whole forsaken generation. Despite
the embracing of darkness, despite the absence of hope
and faith, it is a magnificent elegy, teeming with life.'

Pia Bergström, *Aftonbladet*

'In terms of ambition, few contemporary Swedish authors can compete with Tichý. The same goes for linguistic intensity. His prose rushes forward, roaring with, if you will, dark poetry, hurling its rage at an indifferent present. *Wretchedness* is a furious novel.'

Ann Lingebrandt, *Sydsvenska Dagbladet*

'Authors like Tichý are needed to keep our literature alive. He is drilling frenetically, refusing to neglect the suffering and succeeds in lighting a spark with a linguistic tinder.'

Nils Schwartz, *Expressen*

'In spite of its slimness, this is a huge novel Tichý has written.'

Viktor Malm, *Expressen*

'Andrzej Tichý is an author who, time after time, in language that sings, says something important about contemporary Sweden. Read him.'

Stefan Eklund, *Borås Tidning*

'This is literature. Powerful and moving. And a lament for people with few opportunities to escape "that place" fate has decided for them.'

Inger Dahlman, *Motala Tidning*

'The darkness Tichý evokes has an epic, radiant energy. The frenzy in the narrator's flashbacks forces its way up through the narrative like volcanic continents, full of ruin, tragedy, wretchedness, and a rare, raging and destructive power. It is magnificent, across the board, magnificent.'

Jan-Olov Nyström, *Skånska Dagbladet*

WRETCHEDNESS

WRETCHEDNESS

Andrzej Tichý

Translated by Nichola Smalley

SHEFFIELD – LONDON – NEW YORK

First published in English in 2020 by And Other Stories
Sheffield – London – New York
www.andotherstories.org

Originally published as *Eländet* by Albert Bonniers Förlag, Sweden, in 2016.
Copyright © Andrzej Tichý, 2016

Published by arrangement with Nordin Agency AB, Sweden

Translation copyright © Nichola Smalley, 2020

Quotation from the following sources gratefully acknowledged:

'One' written by James Hetfield and Lars Ulrich. Published by Creeping Death Music (GMR). All Rights Reserved. Used by Permission. 'Shook Ones, Pt. II' by Mobb Deep; 'So Glorious' by Killer Mike; 'Real' by DJ Krush feat. Tragedy Khadafi; 'Free Will and Testament' by Robert Wyatt; 'The Lost Prison Tapes' by Tupac Shakur; *Gravity and Grace* by Simone Weil, translated by Emma Crawford and Mario von der Ruhr (Routledge Classics); *The Cherry Orchard* by Anton Chekhov, translated by Richard Nelson, Richard Pevear and Larissa Volokhonsky (Theatre Communications Group); 'Versiegle mir die Zunge, binde mich' by Hugo Ball (new translation); *Die Flucht aus der Zeit* (Flight Out of Time) by Hugo Ball, for which the translation by Ann Raimes, *Flight Out of Time: A Dada Diary*, (University of California Press) was the source of the paraphrase: 'The skull was the name given to a girl in the nomads' language. The outline of her skeleton showed in her worn features.'

9 8 7 6 5 4 3 2 1

ISBN 9781911508762
eBook ISBN 9781911508779

Editor: Anna Glendenning; Copy-editor: Gesche Ipsen; Proofreader: Sarah Terry. Typeset in Linotype Neue Swift and Verlag by Tetragon, London. Cover design: Sarahmay Wilkinson. Printed and bound on acid-free, age-resistant Munken Premium by CPI Limited, Croydon, UK.

And Other Stories gratefully acknowledge that our work is supported using public funding by Arts Council England and that the cost of this translation was defrayed by a subsidy from the Swedish Arts Council and a grant from the Anglo-Swedish Literary Foundation.

Supported using public funding by

Contradiction alone is the proof that we are not everything. Contradiction is our wretchedness, and the sense of our wretchedness is the sense of reality. For we do not invent our wretchedness. It is true. That is why we have to value it. All the rest is imaginary.

SIMONE WEIL,
GRAVITY AND GRACE, 1947

That last day – a Friday afternoon at the beginning of October – I was waiting for the guitarist and the composer down by the canal, by the gravel track between the police station and the water. I stood there, thinking about the wax plants, whose whitish-pink and perfumed petals had opened overnight, and about some of the lessons I felt I might take away from that morning's practice of a Scelsi piece, which had been as focused as it was fruitful. And just as I was unsuccessfully trying to remember the name of an Italian philosopher who'd written a long and exceptionally deep and incisive essay on Scelsi's work and importance, a guy came up and asked if I could spare any change for the homeless. I felt about in my right pocket and found a twenty-krona note, scrunched up, irregularly folded, which I gave to him. He took it without a word and stuffed it in the pocket of his black jacket, whose fur-edged hood was pulled up, hiding large parts of his head. I was smoking and I could see that he was looking at the cigarette, following it with his eyes. I saw him but I didn't offer him one. I looked back at him, looked him straight in the eye and I wasn't afraid. He was a young guy, really thin, frail, I thought, if he tries anything I'll knock him down no problem. Even if he has a knife or a gun. He was still looking at the cigarette as I brought it to my lips. I took a drag, and then let my hand drift from the lower part of my face down to my stomach, approximately level with my navel, and I saw his eyes follow the movement. I exhaled. Smoke and ember, paper and tobacco. I could have offered him a cigarette, but I didn't think of it. He could have asked, but he didn't. And I saw he was looking at my bike, which was leant against the wooden bench behind me, or perhaps it was a utility box. Then he said he'd been beaten up in the night, the previous night. He said: I don't know where I'm going to sleep and I got beaten up yesterday. He said someone had hit him in the ribs and the face. I looked again and now I saw it, a bruise and a little graze on his left cheek, by his cheekbone. I asked him: who beat you up? He said something I didn't understand. He said a name. His tongue moved in his mouth. I asked why and he said something about them *getting junked too much*. He said: he's a whore. Those words made me flinch a little, as though their aggression was too intimate, and all at once I thought of Robert, a childhood friend I'd recently bumped into, on a sunny day, down by the sea, down by Limhamn Fields, before a five-a-side match. We hadn't seen each other for years. He was big and well built now, no longer the gangly teenager I remembered, and he told me in a neutral tone, with no shame or swagger, that he'd been inside, that he'd stabbed a guy with a screwdriver when he was interrupted doing a robbery. He did a few years, got out and got a job at some factory making optical equipment or whatever. He said it was cool now, it was good to have a job. I told him briefly what I'd been doing the last few years. I mentioned the adult education classes, the

Academy of Music and my life as a freelance musician.
It's cool, I said, adding that I guessed it must be nice to
have a permanent job. He replied that it wasn't permanent. He was on a zero-hours contract. But there's stuff
to do, he said. Then he asked if I went to Prague much. I
said: no, it's been a few years. He said: fucking nice whores
in Prague. I didn't reply. Followed the freshly chalked
touchline with my gaze, over to the corner flag, the little
orange triangle in the high wind. When I looked back at
him he'd also turned away. I don't know what happened.
I think we shook hands and said: well, take it easy, bro,
look after yourself. We went our separate ways. The wind
blew up great clouds from the dry gravel pitches. I looked
after him, saw his shoulder blades and the muscles on
his back and thought, I have to tell someone about this,
but I never have, not even the guitarist or the composer.
I stood looking after him and suddenly remembered how
he'd helped me once during a fight on one of the estates.
I was fighting Carlos, I think about his girl Victoria, she
was standing on one side, flattered I think – I saw her one
night years later when I was buying a burger at the kiosk
on Möllevångstorget, she was working there, making
fries in her Sibylla uniform, pretending she hadn't recognised me – and I had Carlos in some kind of grip so he
couldn't breathe, and his top was pulled up, exposing the
bottom of his back, and then Robi ran up with a lighter
and some kind of spray can, like deodorant or something,
and set light to the gas and burned Carlos on the back.
Only for three or four seconds, but he yelled and I let him
go and he backed away and stood against the brick wall
and we could tell from the look of him that he'd lost, that
he was scared and about to give up. But the thing was

that Carlos was my friend. He was a hard little Chilean. He was smart, a maths geek. He lived with his grandparents, I think because his dad was a user and a drinker – a few times, years later, I thought I saw the dad, sitting on the benches by Värnhemstorget, and every time I had to stifle an impulse to go up and ask what had happened to Carlos, his little Carlito, my friend – and I don't know what was up with his mum. She was Swedish I think, I'm not sure I ever met her. There was some custody thing I think, at least when he was younger, like in primary school. Once, when we were in year one or two, a car came into the turning area by the supermarket, there by the school, what was it, Snödroppsgatan maybe, and someone jumped out and dragged Carlos into the car, right in the middle of break while we were playing our games, playing marbles or whatever, and we thought it was pretty weird that someone could just rock up from nowhere and drag a kid into a car like that, it felt like something out of a film, not reality. But we'd seen it happen. What did it mean? I don't really know what we decided. Several days later Carlos was back, peddling some lie no one believed, and then we never talked about it again. Homes were generally very simple. The houses were usually built of mud or plastered, often with just one room. The houses mostly had flat roofs, where the family could rest, sleep and work. The roofs were made of brushwood, mud and earth. They had to be flattened out after heavy rainfall. Years later I heard he'd been into drugs and hanging out with little kids, getting them to run errands for him so he wouldn't go down, probably, but someone at the school told the kids they shouldn't hang out with him, and then he went to the school and threatened the teachers. I dunno. What can I say? It felt so ridiculous. This thing with the gaze. Or, I dunno, these fantasies, and this thing of not being the first to look away, you know. And if you are it doesn't feel good. What can I say? There's nothing weird about it, actually, even though you might think there is. Me and Robert, who was half Polish, used to hang out with a Polish gypsy called Tony, we called him Montana, yeah, and he went around wearing a suit and you know like gold chains and jewellery and all that shit, he used to have 100-krona notes tucked into the plastic wrapper on his cigarette packets, playin gangsta, as we used to say, and one time I met him by the school – he liked me, you know, I don't know why, maybe because we spoke Polish sometimes and he was too young to understand it didn't mean anything, you know, that the Poles hated him just as much as the Swedes, I dunno – but anyway I ran up to him and he was standing there with this bike and the chain had come off, one of those racing bikes from the eighties, so I said that's easy to fix, just turn it upside down and we'll fix it, but he said no, fuck it, you'll just get dirty, leave it, come on, come with me to my cousin Luciano's place in Kroksbäck, and we walked along and he said you're all right, you can share my fags as we go, and he pulled out a pack of Marlboros, then suddenly he got mad as hell and said he'd lost a 100-krona note he'd had in there, and as we walked along this guy came past, we didn't know him but I'd seen him at school, was in year nine, geeky, Swedish, and as he passes us, Tony says like, hey fix my bike, and the guy says I can't, I don't know how to do it, and Tony says what, what do you mean you don't know how, just put the fucking chain back on man, it's easy, you'll ace it, and the guy, scared out of his wits, is still like, but, but, but I don't know and shit and Tony jumps up and does a roundhouse kick on his head, hits like, the cheek, not really hard, no blood or nothing, but still, I was a bit surprised, and the guy just gets down on his knees, hands shaking, fiddles with the chain, gets his fingers totally black, I said take it easy Tony, but I was scared of him too, everyone was, and in the end the three of us did it together, Tony holding the bike, me turning the pedals and the guy, I think he might have been called Daniel, like the guy with the lion in the Bible or in that song by Elton John, the guy fiddled with the oily chain till it was in place, and he headed off and we smoked a fag and then he cycled off, Tony did, and I walked on and looked sort of lazily for the 100 he might have lost. That wasn't really my style, actually, jumping innocents like that – that's what I thought then in any case, but maybe that was exactly what I did, maybe I thought it was exciting, kind of fun, kind of entertaining, to see someone get jumped without doing anything myself, I don't know – but I liked Tony all the same, there was some kind of bond there, and one time he helped me when I got in a fight with a guy from the fancy part of town, from Bellevue, some rich man's kid (I looked him up years later, by that point he was a pretty famous chef), who jumped in through the window during class, yeah, cos for some lessons I had to take the remedial classes, as they called them, for unruly students, we were in a smaller group and it was a bit quieter actually, but he climbed in and started picking on some little guy called Lars, he was really small for his age, used to take growth hormones and shit, and the other guy, the rich one, he was a year or two older than us, so I got between them and gave it all that, then he got thrown out and then we bumped into one another again and fought for a bit, but some teachers broke it up, and then someone said we should meet by the hills at twelve, and we met there and had a fight, he chipped a bit off my left front tooth, I can still feel the unevenness with my tongue today, like twenty-five years later, and I guess I got in a few punches and a kick or two, enough for him to know it would cost him something to humiliate me, and in the end we got tired and the circle around us thinned out and we stopped fighting and it ended kind of undecided, but the thing was that Tony found out about it later, and a rumour went round that he was gonna kill the rich kid, and you know, everyone knew he was crazy, and we had another mate, Marcin, a Pole, he bumped into the rich kid in a car park, there was a fight, nothing serious, but you know, Marcin was from Rosengård and had a load of friends there, and Tony knew all the gypsies, as we used to say – so all these rumours spread and in the end the rich kid got well freaked out, or else someone snitched, cos in the end the teachers called me and the rich kid in for some kind of peace negotiation, though it was nothing to do with me any more, but now there we were, and we were meant to apologise and shake hands and shit, and I can't remember what they threatened but I shook his hand and he shook mine and I asked Marcin and Tony to back off and they did, and then he became a chef as I said, pretty famous I think, but still a piece of work, you know, I remember he lived up in the villas, drove around on his brand-new fucking MT5, while me and Rodrigo shared a stolen fucking Puch Maxi with a broken front wheel, we nicked it off Hamza who'd nicked it off someone else of course – and it wasn't exactly risk-free, cos the thing was Hamza was totally wild, shot people in the eye with air guns and shit. What can I say? Homes were generally very simple. We used to sit, me and Carlos and the Kassem twins, Robi and a few others, in the stairwells and set light to plastic. Pots, plastic bags, whatever. I don't know why it fascinated us so much. Mostly we talked about the sound of the plastic dripping on the stone steps. Chop, chop, it went, and we called the whole game 'chop-chop'. I think the whole thing started when someone taught us how to make little smoke bombs from ping-pong balls and aluminium foil. You stole a ping-pong ball and some aluminium foil, wrapped the ball in the foil, it had to be smooth, no wrinkles, and then you set fire to it, the foil would burn, the ball would start burning slowly, start giving off a lot of smoke. The smoke made your eyes itch. The houses were normally divided into two sections, one for the humans and one for their animals. The humans lived in a somewhat raised section with a floor of flattened earth. The windows were small and had no glass, and small oil lamps provided light. A peasant farmer's family would have had no furniture, aside from a few rough skins that were rolled out for sleeping on. The woman of the house was responsible for household work – preparing food, cleaning, spinning, weaving and sewing. She also helped out in the fields and the vineyards at times, and she taught the children when they were young. Generally, they ate two meals a day – a light breakfast of bread, fruit and cheese, and an evening meal consisting of meat, vegetables and wine. And so the years passed. He mumbled something about drugs. I asked which drugs and he said:

too much. He said: benzos, speed, horse. Too much. Grain harvest, linen harvest. The early figs ripen. I don't know where I'm going to sleep tonight. Grape harvest. How old are you? Olive harvest. Twenty-four. He inhales. Summer figs, dates. Go now. We'll pray for you. Winter figs, ploughing. Sowing. Lemon harvest. Yet another year has passed. And he, like an idiot, said it was no good. He said: brah, you know . . . it's no good. And I kind of nodded and shook my head all at once, because I knew and didn't know, saying: I know, bro. And then I left. And everything played on in my head. And he, like an idiot, said: it's no good, the life you're living, it's not good, man, you're young and that, and I replied: I know, man, I'm not stupid, and he, like a big brother or maybe a father, no, not a father, then he would have hit me, that's what I was thinking, beaten a little sense into me, as they say, like a real father, but no, and again he said it was no good, he said he'd also *been into that kind of thing*, sounded like a real idiot, but he'd quit, was totally *clean*, totally *squeaky*, and I looked at him, as I would at a brother or something, I swear, and he said: I've got out of selling, got off road, *yani*, I swear, and I said, sort of looked up to him and replied: got off everything, have you? Walking defeated and dirty and deathlike along the edge of the path in a black jacket, hood pulled up. Chapped skin and damp, smoke-infused clothes propping up head and face. Walking, fiddling with a lighter. I replied: yeah, bro, I have kids now, family and a job now, have to take it easy now, and you know . . . it's no good. And then a few years passed and then I went by again and then he looked at me and said: *I'm ashamed of you*, and then *shit you're an embarrassment, man*. I left. And everything played on in my mind, the whole night, whole nights. Then the guitarist came and the composer, they were late and I could see the guitarist had been stressing and he apologised and I said no big deal, and the composer said she thought we still had plenty of time, and we started walking and I was about to say something about the junkie when the guitarist said: do you remember?

The wax plants had blossomed during the night, and in the morning while practising I could see their flowers vibrating. Not – as I at first, a little vainly, imagined – because of the cello, whose strings I was doing my best to manipulate in line with Scelsi's directions (or rather, in line with one of Scelsi's interpreter's directions – he had an underling, a so-called 'negro', who did the notation for him: Tosetti, or whatever his name was), but rather because of the freight train rolling by two or three hundred metres away, making my window and the rest of the building resonate with a weak low-frequency tone, and perhaps I saw something in the junkie's face, something in the whites of his eyes, that made me think about that again, the whitish-pink petals, vibrating and shining stiffly, as dead as they were alive. We walked along the canal and the guitarist said: do you remember that thing we listened to – what was it – maybe fifteen, sixteen, seventeen years ago? That Loren Connors guy. *Airs*? I didn't really hear what he said, I was working hard on not drifting off altogether. Wasn't he called Mazzacane? the composer said. Yeah, right, that's the one, the guitarist said. Yeah, said the composer, as she pulled out a little bag of throat drops, liquorice or mint pastilles or something.

Yeah, I remember it was kind of impressionistic, him just going round and round on some minor chord, kind of thing. She held the bag out to us. The guitarist took one while I shook my head a little. Right, the guitarist said, and moved the little pastille around his mouth with his tongue, which made me think of the junkie's slightly slack, dribbling mouth, maybe he uses open C tuning, and it's almost like he was playing slide but without the slide, just round round round, and all the songs are the same, some pentatonic scale the whole time or something, I think so anyway, and like, it shouldn't work but it does, it doesn't sound as kitsch as it should, and I think it has something to do with the rhythm, that it's kind of irregular, fluid, swaying, you think, just because it's called *Airs*, like the air, but in plural, which is impossible, but it's got nothing to do with that, apparently it has roots in Celtic or Irish harp music, he said, and I tried to say something but sort of couldn't get it out, and I got out a cigarette instead and lit it and tried again to say something but I couldn't, it was as though something had broken, something really small of course, but still, broken, cracked, burst, some little part or thread that was essential to speech, and we walked on the gravel, it crunched and scrunched rhythmically and the composer listened and I was listening and not listening, and the guitarist went on talking about Connors, and Turlough O'Carolan in particular, in like the 1700s, he died in the 1700s at any rate, 1738 I think, and I don't know if he was born in the 1600s, or when it was, I mean, I guess people didn't live as long back then, but anyway, that last piece he wrote, like on his deathbed, was called *Carolan's Farewell to Music*, and that I like, the fact he didn't bid farewell to life, to the world, but to music, and . . . He broke off. I inhaled and said: oh, so he didn't think it would be possible to make music after dying. No, apparently not, the guitarist said, and we went on walking along the canal and I looked down at the gravel, down at the grains of gravel, and it made the noise it does and I felt something, a diffuse pain, and I thought, as though in the background, while I was speaking, whether I should mention something to them. But what? I didn't want to make a big deal out of it. The feeling, this pain that was impossible to locate or describe, was familiar but ungraspable. What could I say to the guitarist and the composer? How could I formulate it? Maybe it can't be explained, maybe it can't be described, talked about, maybe it can't be done, as they say, maybe I shouldn't say anything about it, maybe I should just be quiet, keep on listening, maybe it will pass after a while, that was what I was thinking now, and we walked on, we walked on along the canal, alongside one another, and I heard the composer's voice as I was thinking about Robi's brother, who'd also been inside for something or other, and the corner flag and the cloud of gravel, and my mouth got dry and I breathed and looked up at a tower block in front of us, saw someone moving about up there on the roof, and thought about Copenhagen, where we were headed, to a concert at Vor Frue Kirke, in the cathedral – where Moosmann was going to play *In Nomine Lucis*, among other things – and I thought about Sanne in Copenhagen and I heard the composer's voice but couldn't listen, because I was hearing Robi's voice at the same time and seeing Robi's back receding, getting smaller and smaller, but his voice was just as persistent and rich inside my head. Fucking nice whores,

Robi'd said, and I thought of Sanne, who fell from the fourth floor, somehow she survived that jump, that fall, Sanne, who grew up in Copenhagen Central Station, raised by the johns on Halmtorvet, as she used to say, they were a gang of, I don't know, five or six kids aged thirteen, fourteen who used to hang out together. 'The little match girls' and 'the ugly ducklings', Jane used to call them, she was a psychologist at the supported housing they used sometimes (without really understanding, I think now, what that kind of characterisation, those associations, did to them). They stuck mainly to the central parts of Copenhagen – Vesterbro, Nørrebro, Østerbro and Christiania – but occasionally I visited Sanne in a little apartment in Ishøj where her brother lived. I met them in Christiania, on the way to Aarhus, Hamburg, Marseille or Istanbul, and we recognised each other immediately, that's how I remember it. We – failed abortions, as she put it – all found ourselves in the same place: a hard, lurching place we'd come to to escape this or that, various hazes, various forms of violence, to disappear inside something, another haze, a numbness, a repose. We wandered about at night, slept in stairwells, on benches and in parks, in churchyards and the homes of various more or less lousy people we bumped into by chance, or because they had something we needed, money mostly. Sanne. Nicko, Wotan. Vivi. Fox, you trippy fuck. And I noticed the guitarist had asked me something, so I looked at him, mumbled a few words and gave a nod as he repeated: it *shouldn't* work, but it *does*, in spite of everything, it's really good, you know, evasive, subtle melodies, and I thought about the junkie's ribs, and I thought of the pain and I thought of all the hundreds or even thousands of times I'd stood there, practising body blows in all those different gyms, with condensation dripping from the ceiling, onto the floor, onto us, where we threw punches at a bag or at mitts, threw punches and drove in punches, and I thought of the three times I'd thrown a really solid punch – decisive blows, as they say – once at a plain-clothes cop, though I didn't know he was a cop and he didn't do anything afterwards because he was on his own and because he was embarrassed that I'd brought him down with a single blow, and once at some mouthy guy in a club, and the last time at a racist who picked a fight with me on a night bus – and all three times were really successful, proper solid punches few could get up from, and every time, all that happened was I lifted my left hand and touched their face, with a little jerk, but lightly, very lightly, not a blow, almost a caress, so they would lift their arms in defence in a kind of reflex, expos-ing their body, their ribs, their spleen, and so I could get in position for the body blow, that is, with my right hip and shoulder back a little, and then just drive it in full power, from the legs, from the hip, just whip it in with the elbow at just the right angle and pointing up a little, and see the guys sink down with broken ribs and that expression on their faces that says: *hey, wait, what's hap-pening now?* – but I was thinking too of that time I got a cracked rib after getting kicked in the chest, and that pain, I recall it so clearly, those breaths, so shallow, so careful so as not to cause more pain, that absolutely horrific pain, and the contradiction of feeling it when you breathe, which you can't stop doing, you have to breathe after all, you have to live after all, and I didn't hear what the guitarist said and I thought I had to sort myself out, pull myself together, so I focused my gaze and said: *Airs*? As in the stuff we breathe? You have to live, after all, I thought again. Yeah, as in air, the composer said. Like shoes, don't you have some of those? Yeah, look, she pointed at my shoes, at my feet, down at the gravel. Like Nike Airs, she said. Plural, air in plural. And the guitarist said: yeah, that's right. Or in a way at least. Air or ayre, it means like, song or melody, and it's actually connected to aria, which comes from like air or aer, but then . . . he lost his thread a moment . . . I mean, it's patterns, he said, it's that, he almost stammered, it's that, that, that, that the music is there in the oscillations, there, there's, there's, there's nothing strange about it. Even if you might think – Now I interrupted him. Yeah, I said, sound is air after all, and . . . or I mean . . . I felt suddenly tired and thirsty, like a hangover, even though I hadn't had anything to drink. Well, the composer said, not really, but OK, like oscillations in the air, pressure . . . I yawned. Changes in pressure, you know, it's to do with the production values, or with the echo, the resonance, the production, the reverb, I don't know how much you mute the strings when you play the harp, I don't think you do, though I guess you have to, in fact, maybe it's necessary, I mean, maybe it's obvious . . . When spring comes, another year has passed, and we travel past yet another lake. Everything is grass, birches, sky. House after house after house. Birches, sky, another year has passed. I can hardly believe it's true. We've lived yet another year. The large rooms are divided up into several smaller rooms, with no regard paid to ventilation or light. The amount of rent was decided by the size of the room and the distance from the street. Soon enough the whole house filled up, from basement to loft, by tenants who lived from hand to mouth, morally loose, with careless habits, a lost people, just as obscene as beggars. It's like Robert Wyatt says: *Be in the air, but not be air, be in the no air*, the guitarist said with a muted laugh, and I searched for the tune a while, and then it came, *Had I been free, I could have chosen not to be me*, but I didn't say anything, let it play on in my mind. What kind of spider understands arachnophobia? Yeah, I see now, he said, what it means . . . But I didn't hear. I was somewhere else, because that thing about the ribs made me think about Kiko and the last time I'd met him, his books and that last night, the night that started at Kiko's flat and finished god knows where. It was the first time I'd been to his place. I took the metro there, it was early evening, after work. I found the street with the help of a crumpled little map I'd got from Argo, I think he'd torn it out of a free paper. I got into the yard via a rickety wooden door covered with tags and shreds of old posters. In the entrance it was dark and damp and I clearly remember the heavy smell of rubbish and old piss, which made me raise a hand to my face and quicken my step. The yard consisted of cracked, moss-covered asphalt and a two-metre-high red-brick wall. On the wall someone had sprayed a goal with a stick man for a goalie, and in one corner was a rack for beating mats. Four children about ten years old were standing next to it. I looked around. There were three stairwells. I turned to the kids. Excuse me, do you know where Kiko lives? They looked at me, two boys and two girls. Francisco? Short guy with dreads? He means the nigger, one of the boys said quietly to the other. I suddenly saw he had a large kitchen knife in his hand and the other boy was holding out his arm with the inside upwards, upon which two long cuts were bleeding slowly. Hey, what the hell is this? I said. He can't feel anything, said the older girl quickly. But what the hell are you doing? I asked again, and moved closer. The boy with the bloody arm said: it's true. I've got no feeling in my arm. His nose was blocked. I could see a little drip of snot in one of his nostrils. We're just kidding about, said the boy with the knife. What the fuck do you care. You're a fresh one, kiddo, I said, taking hold of the wrist of the hand holding the knife. Watch out you don't get a slap. Fuck you, you fucking creep. The boy tore himself away as he dropped the knife and spat in my face before running out through the main gate, which slammed loudly behind him. Having instinctively turned my face away, I wiped the saliva from my cheek and looked at the other children. The older girl shook her head a little. You shouldn't have touched him. Adults shouldn't touch children. The boy with no feeling looked at the blood running down his arm, the back of his hand, between his knuckles, the middle finger and the ring finger, and dripping down onto the ground. Are you OK? I said. I don't have any feeling in my arm, the boy said again. No, but you're bleeding, for fuck's sake. You need to put a plaster on it or a bandage or something. Why do you care so much, who the fuck are you? the girl said. I threw my arms up and nodded. Yeah, that's a good question. A really good question. What do I care? I turned my back to them, walked back to the gate and muttered something about them being totally fucked up, tried to sort of shake them off me, but I looked back immediately and asked over my shoulder: do you know where Kiko lives, or not? C, the girl said, pulling out a tissue. Second floor. Thanks a lot,

I said, with as much sarcasm as I could muster. You're welcome, *blatte*, she replied quietly. The boy grimaced as he gave me the finger. I stopped, intending to turn back and carry on arguing, but, realising it was pointless, clenched my jaw briefly and headed for door C instead. I walked up the stairs, saw Kiko's name and rang the doorbell. Kiko opened up. All right Cody? What's goin on? Nothing much, Kiko said. Playing PlayStation. I walked into the hallway. OK. What game? *Resident Evil*. I nodded and grinned. Got stuck in Raccoon City, right? As per usual mate, Kiko said with a grimace. Shit, sick fucking kids on your estate, man, I said, hanging up my jacket. I know. Don't talk to them. They're totally messed up. Racist too. We went into the living room. The blinds were down, it was dark and smelled of smoke. A big lava lamp and the glow from the TV. Yeah, one of them anyway. It's just cos his brother's a skinhead. But he's not dangerous. Just stupid. Plays Skrewdriver and all this racist Oi! shit so the whole yard shakes with it. He laughed and sat down in the armchair. I went over to the lava lamp, leaned over and followed a red, amoeba-like clump with my finger. I normally answer with N.W.A and my speakers are better so I always win. I don't know. It sort of feels like they need their heads smashing in. Perhaps we're too kind to the little bastards. Kiko started playing again. I sat on the sofa, looked at the zombies filling the screen. Bloody arms, like the little guy with no feeling. Though one time he actually got a gun out, Kiko said as he played. The brother or the little guy? The little guy. You're kidding. I swear. A Beretta, with the serial number scratched out. He must have got it off the dwarf, you know, Carlos. The only guy I know who's cold enough to hook little kids up with that kind of shit, Kiko said, shaking his head. Do you know about that stuff? Like which one? Beretta and all that, brands and shit? Not really. I just know that brand cos I had one a while back. Replica, but still. Sold it when I bought the Akai sampler. What happened with the little dude then? No, nothing. When I didn't back off, he did. As usual. *As usual*, I laughed. What the fuck, don't play gangsta. He asked if I wanted to play a little *RE*. I said no. There was fruit on the coffee table. I asked if I could have an apple. Course, he said. Have a red one, they're amazing. We talked while he played. I saw he had a book on the table and I peered at it. Edgar Allan Poe. Kiko said he liked Poe. The stories. The poems felt a bit old-fashioned. He'd been given a copy by his sister when he was in hospital in London. I asked why he was in hospital. He told me he'd been jumped by racists in Seville. And he'd stabbed one of them in the stomach. He didn't know what happened to the other guy. He'd got concussion and broken ribs and a punctured lung. Then in London the wound in his lung had reopened or something and he was brought in again. He said the pain was indescribably awful. He just wanted more and more morphine the whole time. But when the pain finally disappeared it was pretty nice to lie there and trip out to Poe's stories. It was then he realised he liked reading. He went to a library and was surprised when the librarian, this old lady, sixty-odd, pulled out a load of books on zombies and old German poems about corpses and stuff. I asked about the attack and he told me it happened at night outside a train station. I asked if he carried a knife. Not any more, he said. But it was different there. You had to carry a knife with you in Spain, even if you didn't want to, because Spain was heaving with sick racists, he said. Fucked up, that is, I said. But you know, that Poe guy was a racist too, Kiko said. Everyone's a fucking racist. You know what she called me, I said. The little girl in the yard. No, he said, and turned off the game and the TV. What? *Blatte*. She said: *You're welcome, blatte*. Really? Shit. That's sick. I laughed. Right? You know how long it's been since I heard that? What? That long? To my face, I mean, yeah, it's been a long time. Really? I swear. God, do you remember the first time? I remember it in detail, man. Nah, I don't. OK, I can't remember the year, but it was at a football camp, like '88, '89, '90, something like that. So you were like ten, eleven? Shit, that old? I swear, it was the first time. It was at football camp. Me and someone, I don't remember who, maybe Besart, someone else, we were winding up these older guys, taking their ball and shit. Then one of them, his name was Magnusson or Magnus or something, whatever, then he said *fucking blattar* to us. I'd never heard it so I didn't get it. But then I asked someone. And they said: it means foreigner, immigrant, dirty wog, you know, though I hadn't heard that then either. And I couldn't let it go of course, so when I went past this guy Mange, or maybe his name was Tobbe, I slammed him in the chest, or the stomach maybe, with everything I had. Without a word . . . all psycho? Yeah, yeah, totally silent, just: *bam*. So what happened? What happened? He was almost a foot taller than me. He looked at me and punched me full in the face so I got a split lip. Then I got a massive caning from the trainer and later from my mum for getting in fights. Catastrophe. Yeah. Totally. A thick lip and total disgrace for having stood up for myself. Know what? I was at a camp like that once too. I was about ten, twelve, too, maybe a bit older. These neo-nazis came along and were gonna smack us up. What, adults? Yeah, yeah, they had cars and shit, motorbikes. Drove up late one night when it was dark. The camp leaders and older kids chased them off, but, you know, we were shitting ourselves. Course. Thought they were gonna lynch us, brah. Sick times. Yeah. Really, really sick. Think about them all. What are they doing now? Think about it. Guys like that, frightening kids. Honestly. I don't wanna know, I said, I hope they don't exist any more. No, Kiko said, but they're probably around. They're probably politicians now, and soon they'll take over everything. We sat quietly a while. Then Kiko told me, out of nowhere, that he had a son somewhere he wasn't allowed to see, the mother didn't want anything to do with him. He showed me a photo of a tiny baby. It's a fucking old picture, he said. He's five now. I haven't seen him for three years. I'm not allowed to see him. Why, I asked. I don't know, he told me. I didn't say anything. Kiko started rolling a spliff. It's complicated, he said. Complicated? I said. He didn't reply. Damn, I didn't know you were a dad, I said, and tried to sound happy. We smoked. Really oily black kush from the Zambian by Metro. The guy we bought New York Diesel from? Exactly, him. It hit me hard and Kiko put on DJ Screw, who I'd never heard. 'Still D.R.E.' from *Freestyle Kings*, bro. I'm spinning out, this is so heavy. Neither of us could speak, I looked at Kiko with eyes like tiny cracks, the muscles in my face soft. Shit, I'm spilling out across the floor, man. Pff, I said, pointing at my forehead. Suddenly he took the remote, put the music on mute and looked at me with a really pained expression. You know, he said, my mamma sold ganja in Córdoba when I was little. I didn't respond, it was all so weird. We never used to say 'ganja' – that was the kind of thing the wannabe Rastas said. I tried to think, but everything was somehow drawn out. What did he mean? I didn't know what to say, my tongue was stuck fast to the roof of my mouth. I just said, is that true, feeling as twisted as the music. As though waves were passing through my body and driving my flesh down towards the ground, down towards the dark-blue carpet, which I was scraping my toes against, where brown tobacco flakes and small columns of ash lay where I'd dropped them. My mouth was dry but I managed to gather a small quantity of saliva which I put on the tip of my index finger, then bent down and touched, as carefully as I could, the ash so it stuck and lifted from the floor. I brushed my finger against the edge of the ashtray and wiped it on my trousers. When I looked at the carpet again it looked the same, dark blue, with tobacco flakes and lumps of ash, cylindrical, grey marl. Hadn't I just removed them? I was drawn down again, my hand carried on wiping my finger against my trousers. Kiko blew out a deep toke and squinted. I swear, he said. Heavy, I said. I looked at him and saw he'd got stuck somewhere, he was still squinting and his eyebrows were raised in two high arches. Two arches, two lines and a mouth that said the same thing again, kind of mechanically, as though he was practising a line. *My-mamma-sold-ganja-in-Córdoba-when-I-was-little*. The words echoed in my brain: *mamma ganja Córdoba*. Then I laughed: Kiko, for fuck's sake. I don't know where Córdoba is. He too, laughing: *en Andalucía, puto*. He put the sound on, the bass flowed in again and we listened, so stoned we even forgot it was time to roll another. Then we left and went to meet Soot,

Dima, Becca, Sanne – and the others, Adi, Olga, Ponyboy, Lajos. That was the last night and we never said goodbye. Soot, I thought. Soot, goddamn Soot. The guitarist pointed at a tower block and said something. I looked up and saw two figures moving about on the roof, at least ten, twelve floors up. But a few seconds passed before I realised that, aside from an interjected *look*, what he was talking about had nothing to do with the figures. But Langille, the composer said, she's done loads of interesting things too and those records they made together are really good. You know, sometimes it makes me think about Colette Magny actually, have you heard her interpretations of Artaud, where she shouts and makes a load of noise and howls and rages? Totally fantastic, really. Not because Langille does all that, but there's a tone there, a, how can I put it, like a *Stimmung*, if you get what I mean. The composer looked at me. Speaking of *Stimmung*, how's it going with the microtones? When I didn't answer for a few seconds, she added: *pun intended*. Soot fell, I thought. I got off lightly.

The way the wax-plant flowers moved, those small movements, that trembling, that gentle vibrating, like an echo
of the moving strings, combined with the low-frequency
tone, the rumble – all that lingered in my consciousness
as I saw the newly built tower block and the figures on
its roof, with the railway tracks and rail yard in the background, all while I tried to say something to the guitarist
and the composer about Scelsi and my microtonal work.
We walked towards the central station to take the train
to Copenhagen, to Vor Frue Kirke and the Moosmann
concert, and I pushed my bike with both hands now, and
when we crossed the road I looked around and thought
for a moment that I couldn't orient myself, that I didn't
recognise the setting, and I thought the roundabout must
be newly built too, the same with the fence and the
benches, and we walked along the canal, between the
water and the tracks, on newly laid tarmac, and I felt the
bike moving differently: lighter, smoother, and our shoes
made no noise, or almost none at least, and the guitarist
said: was it some special instrument he had for that?
Yeah, I said. Well, I don't know about special, it was something called an ondiola, a kind of Italian version of a
clavioline, I think, that early synth. The composer said

something about microtonal potential and the guitarist started going on about Tolgahan Çoğulu's custom-built instruments with their moveable frets, and I was listening partly, half, as though dazed, or absent-minded, lost in thought as they say, looking at the graffiti, thinking about Soot, of course, again. Homeless, face pressing against the ground. The guitarist and the composer were talking fast, so fast I couldn't keep up, I'd barely had time to understand the words, their import, before the next salvo came. A lot of people have experimented with microtonal tunings, the composer said, students of Pauline Oliveros, who was doing that kind of thing too. She turned to me: she's listened to Scelsi a fair bit, I reckon. Bro, I can't do it, I can't take any more. Riverbed. Structures like mudbanks, levees, oxbow lakes and cut-off channels out in the delta. And I thought, again: I got off lightly. And Soot, I heard him say cherry orchard. Just like that. Got off lightly. That place, if it is a place. It is a place, and it's a movement. It's a bus on a roundabout. It's a bus moving forward and round, it sways and I brace my body, grip the handhold, the bus judders, vibrates, the driver accelerates, our bodies want to fall, outwards, backwards, and I grip the handhold and look up at the roof. And Alvin Lucier, that piece for cello and vases? Have you played it? I mean it's a completely different thing, right, but it sounds the same, if I'm not mistaken? I thought about Soot, and another writer who'd recently died, hit by a commuter train. Not that I knew him or anything, I just read about it and saw it before me, as I'd seen Soot die again and again in my imagination, even though it had never happened to him, even though I knew he looked after himself, that he was careful. I'm careful, he always said. I'm careful. But you can never be careful enough. At four in the morning that other guy died and he left a final tag behind him, a final little dash of colour. No, I said, no, but I've heard Charles Curtis play it. It's really nice, yeah. I looked at the front wheel of the bike, turning, the spokes that vanished and appeared, vanished and appeared with the movement. So still and lovely, I said. Sure, I guess there are links. But the differences are probably bigger, at least if you're playing the pieces. And I started thinking about the black-and-white moiré pattern on the sleeve and about Scelsi's work with the golden ratio. What differences were there? Arithmetic, geometry, harmony. Wasn't everything mathematics, or at least patterns, repetition, variation? But Soot, I thought. Soot, that's what we called him, that was his tag, and I thought about that place, what was it, twenty years ago, that roundabout, when I sat on the bus and the sun was rising and I saw bloodstains on shoes, swollen knuckles, but the clouds and the sky too, white and blue, just as something brown became green and yellow in the grass in the middle of the roundabout we were passing, the bus swayed and I was pulled out towards the sides, I spent my time on the city's southern periphery, not far, not far at all from the little allotments where people grew, and maybe still do grow, mint and garlic, thyme and parsley, carrots and radishes and candy-striped beetroot, probably not that far from the fenced-off cherry orchards I'd never in my life seen – *The cherry orchard's been sold!* Soot said, and yeah, we called him Soot, even though he was called something else, cos that was his tag, and he liked to say those words, *cherry orchard*, and I wonder how long he remembered it, how often he said those words towards the end, if he sat somewhere, a fucked-up bloody tramp of a junkie who everyone abandoned, especially the ones who loved him, if he sat and repeated the words to himself or to someone else, if anyone listened to a ghost like that, *cherry orchard*, I don't know why, I think it was just the sound, that he enjoyed saying it, that he just liked to say *cherry orchard*, that he enjoyed saying *Kirschgarten*, that he liked saying *körsbärsträdgården*, that it gave him something: saying *višňový sad*, or *livada de vişini*, or *cseresznyéskert*, or *višne bahçesi*, I don't know, that there was something about the different languages, the different sounds, the prosodic fragments, I don't know, perhaps it was just that he knew a line from something in school, I don't know why he knew it. *Was the cherry orchard sold? Yes*, he said. *Who bought it? I bought it. I bought it*, he said. *Wait, ladies and gentlemen, please, my head's in a fog, I can't speak*, he said – not far, not far at all from motorway bridges, figs and quinces and kitchen windows with watercress and forest glades where dense carpets of wood sorrel still cover the ground, and I don't know, but all that's going on as the bus sways its way around the roundabout, I'm gripping the grey handhold, bracing my body and looking out through a slightly scratched windowpane, up at the clouds, yes, the white, it's a circular motion, but it's more than that, another motion, a centrifugal force, we drive round and round, but also out and out, I'm on my way round and out, far out, in the same way I'm on the way out, far out, far away from the flickering strip lights of the station, away from everything I've done and away from Dima and Hex and the kids in the squat and all that, and I'm being drawn out, into the south of the city, where I've lived, on the southern periphery, where the city meets the fields, where the city meets the hill, where everything gets bigger in some way, or maybe smaller, like when you zoom out I mean, so everything gets bigger as it gets smaller, you get me, Soot? Like that, just like that, like when you zoom out, everything gets smaller and bigger, bigger and smaller. You get it, Soot? You were proud of that, or – how can I put it – you liked, in any case, to emphasise that: the origin, the source, despite the fact that a conventional pride of place was impossible for us, let alone national pride, in the event we should be interested, since neither we nor our parents ever lived in the same place for more than one or two, maximum three, four years, we always left every place and we were always newcomers to a place, as soon as we stopped being newcomers, as soon as we were no longer strangers in a place, in a community, then we left that community, that place, that location, and now the bus is swaying and I'm pushed out and round, round and out, and you know, I think, when I think of you Soot, I often start talking to myself, I raise my voice, and stand alongside myself and start talking, or I stand in front of myself and start talking, as though I were Soot, as though I were another, and I'm ashamed, but I brush off the shame, try to ignore the narcissism, I start talking, I am Soot, I rock back and forth, suck my teeth, I am Soot, I chew, I talk, I look you in the eye, I suck my teeth and spit, I open my mouth and say something, I'm constantly moving, cracking up, I talk about anything at all, about sandpits, about knives, about miserable filthy clothes, anything, really, or almost anything anyway, about stolen silver jewellery, about gymnastics, about overgrown parks, about how I found several kilos of white powder, packed in plastic bags and taped with brown tape, when I was out playing in that clump of trees we called a forest, out by Tygelsjö, behind the water tower, do you remember Cody, when I was seven, eight years old and Mum rang the police, and they came and collected the bags, they didn't say anything, but I reckon it was amphetamine, and of course we could have sold it and made nuff cash, but Mum didn't know anything about that kind of thing, and even if she had known she never would have done it, and it was probably good she didn't, cos someone probably would have found out, and then we would have had some speed-mafia Pole on our backs, this is the kind of thing I say out loud to myself, I say: Cody, listen, you get me Cody, that's how it was back then, there's so much I could tell you about that, about those areas, the southern parts of these cities, so much, almost too much, about the zones in the south where the hate burns bright, about all the stuff we've sprung from, too much, I say, Cody, Cody, Cody, this kind of chat always makes me think of funerals, Cody, you know, it always makes me think about the dead, it always makes me walk with them, walk beside them, as though I were already one of them, as though we were on the way to yet another of those funerals, yet again, and it's nothing, just there and just then, it means nothing, we don't even know who's being put in the ground, who's in the coffin. Who is it Cody? I don't know, and it's nothing, this, nothing, just a few steps, one leg in front of the other, lungs breathing for themselves, eyes seeing, ears hearing, by necessity, it lives, this body, by necessity, it moves, in need, on the way to yet another funeral, by necessity yet another, but it's not mine, not Ponyboy's, not Lalik's, not Darry's, no, they just fell asleep, and if you open your mouth out it runs, like after getting a tooth knocked out, a funeral, pulled down towards the ground, sunk into the ground, it just runs out, these funerals and these people and this wretchedness, I'm drawn to it, but not to my own, not Blerim's, not Shaban's, or Chabanne's, not Jovan's, or Jonny's, not String's, not Vlora's, not Wotan's, Ahmed's or Aren's, not Nitwit's, Benny's, Danish's, no, they're just sleeping, their names fall, run out of your mouth, but it's not their funerals this is about, I don't know, I'm just moving forward, looking up at what looks like a pink sky with mother-of-pearl-adorned party horns or whatever, or dark stars, or whatever, and all against my will, it's not my intention, it's *against* my will, *against my intentions*, you get what I'm saying, Cody? The will to shut my mouth is stronger, because the sounds that come out of my open mouth have no meaning, and because, seen from some kind of objective perspective, I intend to keep quiet about everything, because I know there's no meaning in it, and believe me, the impulse to keep my trap shut is strong, the impulse to keep quiet about the funerals, to stop saying names like Erik, Rodde, Elna, Solmaz and Marcin, to let all that go and fall silent forever, that impulse is strong, but it's like after a tooth has been knocked out, you know, your mouth is full of it and it has to run out, cos – this I know, cos I was there when Laila, in pure desperation, cut her tongue out – swallowing blood in such large quantities is no good for the body, cos the body, the stomach, can't handle it, it's too much iron or something, you start feeling ill, you get nauseous, you get sick, and now my mouth is full of it, of that taste of iron and names and places, of events and movements, of memories and images, I have a mouth full of the tongue she cut off, I have a head full of blood, I see it the whole time, I have waking dreams about it in the day and I dream about it at night, my head is full of it, Cody, I have a mouth full of blood, I have a mouth full of earth, I have a mouth full of you, I have a mouth full of your ears and your mouth, I have a mouth full of your sealed lips, which are hard when they press against my lips, as though they want to bite me, I have a mouth full of foam, I suck on my teeth and blood comes, I eat earth full of worms that tie themselves in knots in my throat, earth and gravel that scrapes against my palate, my mouth sinks in, contorted into grimaces, stuck through with teeth that bite into and consume it, I have a mouth full of figures, like that poster, who was it that had it on their wall, alongside 2Pac, Hendrix, Marley, Cobain or something. Not Ville, or whatever his name was, not him, my mouth full of earth now, I don't mean Willy D, or whatever he was called, the Greenlander, his mum was a childminder, not him, Eskimo, that's what we called him, the kids crawled around screaming on a filthy rug in one room, he couldn't say S, I think that was it, and not the Albanian, what was his name, everyone said he was gay, but I don't know, not that guy Johnny, I don't know which country he was from, Africa somewhere, not him, so who was it, come on Cody, maybe some *suedi*, not that Turkish girl either, you know, years later I figured out that they weren't Turks after all, they were like Christian Armenians, or Assyrians, or Syrians or something, I don't know, but imagine all those years with everyone chatting shit, we used to go on about smirking Turks and Turks being jerks and all that, everyone said they were rich, that their parents were strict and used to hit them, I dunno, they had to go to university and if they couldn't go to university, start their own business straight away, some were like that, a lot of Iranians, but we didn't have any Iranians, you know, it was mostly Yugos, Chileans, Hungarians, Roma, Albanians and Poles, no Finns, or maybe a few, Arabs from different countries, Turks, Afghans, Somalis, a few Russians, a load of dropout Swedes, yeah yeah OK I'm gonna shut up soon, I don't want to talk bout it either, I just wanna say I started thinking about that guy, if it was him, with that poster, you know, a soldier dying, who gets shot down, from behind, he's falling, dropping his gun, caught just so, in the air, mid-fall, and then it says: *Why?* Do you remember, do you remember us laughing, we creased up, why did he have that picture, his name was Deniz, yeah, he was in care, and fuck it, I can say it to you, but my mouth is sinking inside itself, twisted into grimaces, stuck through with teeth that are biting it to pieces and consuming it, but that's the image I have in my mouth, a poster, white background, black print, a picture of a dying soldier, shot down, dropping his gun and falling and then it says: *Why?* and now I know, man, it's on my tongue, in my mouth, I know we listened to Bob Marley and it was at Deniz's place, that home is in my mouth, that children's home, the community home, it was there, over his bed, that he had that poster, and I don't know, but I remember we sat there listening and he showed me the articles his brother had cut out and saved, and I remember seeing the words *RUBBISH DUMP*, so now I have those newspaper articles in my mouth too, and I have to chew on them, the letters and the pictures, I have to chew those fucking pictures and those fucking letters, those fucking words, cos it didn't just say *RUBBISH DUMP*, it said more than that, it said much more, there were so many words, they were black on white, and the words were *HUMAN* and *RUBBISH DUMP*, those are the words I have in my mouth, man, it's those goddamn fucking words I have in my fucking goddamn mouth, Cody, *HUMAN* and *RUBBISH DUMP*, and you know, my dad said to me that now we've come to *PARADISE*, but in the paper they wrote that it was a *HUMAN RUBBISH DUMP* and that it was a catastrophe and it was 1982 we moved there, to *paradise*, I think, but it was 1985 when they wrote about *the human rubbish dump*, they wrote the suburb of Holma has become a catastrophe district, a *human rubbish dump*, they wrote, Holma has become the part of the city where almost everyone with problems gets relocated, with the blessing of social services, this is not the *Evening Post*'s harsh judgement of a pile of concrete, they wrote, no, this is what the people who live there think about their own neighbourhood, they wrote, and then they wrote that the *Evening Post* has spent a week wandering around Holma, we've met the addicts, the immigrants, the young people who like beating people up, and they wrote that they'd met the embattled idealists who wanted change in Holma, *the idealists who hope it isn't too late*, they wrote, and we'd only been there a short while, but it could already be too late, and others, like Rodde, Elna, Solmaz and Marcin, and fucking loads of others, *hadn't even arrived yet* but it was *already too late*, it could already be too late you see, despite the fact that some of them hadn't even been born, and then we had headlines like *KEEP SWEDEN SWEDISH* and *NO LONGER OUR HOME* and *KNIVES IN OUR BACKS* and *PYROMANIA* and *GRASS FIRES*, it was a special kind of poetry, a rank, shrill song about our childhood, steeped in *Geschäftsgeist*, a poem about our lives in capitals and bold type, with words like *TWO WORLDS* and *SEVEN IN TEN IMMIGRANTS* and *FORCED TO TAKE IN* and *TERRIFYING FACTS* that they repeated for increased impact, *TERRIFYING FACTS* and *THOSE WHO CAN, ESCAPE*, and it's that image I have in my mouth, a photograph of some dark, threatening figures, some teenagers they'd shot in silhouette in front of a corner shop, in silhouette in the dark, that image, and I guess I didn't know anything about it at that time, or at least very little, cos I wasn't one of those kids who got to stand and pose in front of the photographer's lens, I wasn't one of those kids who got to stand there boasting about roundhouse kicks and butterfly knives to a reporter from the *Evening Post*, a reporter so bursting with poetry and lyricism and eloquence and black ink and *Geschäftsgeist* that poetry positively ran out of *his* mouth, like blood, free from violence, blood that came from a good heart, yeah blood, like after a tooth has been knocked out, but in his mouth, and it ran down onto his notepad and then ran onto the presses where it was spread across paper, then cut to shape and stapled together and sent into the world again where it was sucked up into people's brains via their eyeholes, via their pupils, as though they were fleas, ordinary house fleas, ordinary human fleas, as though their ability to read was the proboscis and the newspaper, the very paper it was printed on, was the skin, which they attached themselves to with small but incredibly strong hooks, and the contents, the meaning, the very sense of it, was the bloodily black poetry that had run out of the reporter's mouth, and the blood that, through that

parasitic act, that outwardly, bodily parasitic act, forced
its way out and into their bodies, out into their limbs, in
roughly the same way and in the same order as a baby
develops the ability to move, its gross motor skills and
its fine motor skills, that's to say, first into its eyes, via
the proboscis, and then out into the face, and down into
the neck, then the arms, down into the trunk, and last
of all down the legs and out into the feet, right out into
the toes, as they say, the whole way out and the whole
way down, from top to toe, as they say, and when the
people then moved, when they went about their business,
when they woke and ate breakfast, when they showered
and got dressed, when they left the cosy confines of their
homes, as they say, well, the darkness was always there,
and then, when they threw themselves out into the world,
free and full of confidence and courage and *Geschäftsgeist*, well, then the bloodily dark poetry leaked out into
the atmosphere, like an invisible, scentless gas, more or
less, and when it came back to us then, when we breathed
it in, we too were filled with it, we who'd never even been
there, even I who knew nothing about that stuff, I who
wasn't one of those teenagers, I who was more of a little
brother to those teenagers, or a neighbour, or a school-
mate, the one they frightened when I walked up with my
mind full of childish ideas, playful dreams and wild
hopes, the kind of thing that would soon be beaten out
of me in roughly the same way you toilet-train a cat,
and in that way the outwardly parasitic act has become
an inwardly parasitic act, the darkly bloody poetry
that originated in our own actions, filled our bodies
roughly the way a tapeworm occupies space in a body,
living and growing in the gut, living on our shit, catching

in us, with hooks and suckers, you get me Cody, it's that kinda thing I have in my mouth, I have worms like that in my mouth, with hooks like that and suckers like that, I chew them, I have guts in my mouth, I carry my own guts in my mouth, and I guess that's why I could never make sense of it all in my head, cos you know my dad had told me that now we'd come to *paradise*, and I knew it was the richest land in the world, but in the paper they wrote it was a human *rubbish dump* and it was a catastrophe, and I dunno, it was 1982 we moved there I think, but it was 1985 when they wrote *human rubbish dump*, and so I guess it must have been, big deal, and what can you make on a rubbish dump, well, you make nothing and you make chaos, that's about it, and then you laugh at the adults who break down in front of you and cry from the frustration and the misdirected empathy, or what can I say, nothing and chaos, as I said, there was nothing more to be done, there was nothing, nothing was something, and the thing that actually was something, it was chaos, it smelled of booze, cat's piss, sweat and full ashtrays, the thing that was something, it hurt, it was that laugh, the fact that you knew it was some kind of weapon, that being able to laugh at everything and say fuck it all, bro, like I give a shit, there's nothing you can do to me that's worse than what I go home to every night, it's just chaos, bro, and that was that, big deal, and now I think about it, I'm mostly just surprised that we didn't do worse things, that we didn't burn more things down, that we were pretty moderate, just set fire to the grass and the nursery and that little shed by the garage and a few cars and a motorbike, some shed over by the car park, but never the school and never our own houses, even though we tried a couple of times, or that I didn't beat Danne to death when he said we were dumpster divers, because even if everyone knew it was a human rubbish dump, this place, you didn't wanna look like a tramp, so yeah, I beat the shit out of Danne when he said we were dumpster divers, which I guess we were, to be fair, you know, but it doesn't matter, or I mean, it *didn't* matter, he shouldn't have said it, it wasn't something he should be saying, you know, but it was true, it happened now and then, it happened that Mum called us and said she'd found a new container and we went down to the back yard and unlocked our bikes and pedalled off to some trash-filled metal box somewhere or other, in Bellevue, Kulladal, Gröndal or Ärtholmen, where people threw away things that weren't totally broken, that hadn't fallen apart, not completely anyway, things that could still be used, things that could be fixed, repurposed, used in some way or other, and one of us, or two of us, or all three, depending on whether we had to keep watch or not, jumped into the dumpster and lifted out junk and trash and looked for things that worked, and we were ashamed, it was that whole thing with the human rubbish dump and shit again, you know what I mean I think, and sometimes we didn't find anything, and sometimes we found something, and if we happened to find something we could take home and make use of we got to feel ashamed every time we looked at the thing, cos every time we came into a room and looked at a lamp or a curtain or a chair or a rug, we knew that thing, that toaster, that tray, that juice beaker, it had come out of a dumpster, and we'd dived for it, and that meant we were dumpster divers, no doubt about it, once and for all, and it was the same with the things I'd nicked, the stuff I'd pinched, like that radio I took when we broke into the nursery, when Carlos fell down through the skylight and I jumped down after him and he sprained his foot and I gashed my hand, and I nicked the radio, I stole it and lied to Mum that I'd found it in the bin rooms on some estate, or in a dumpster, that someone had thrown it out, they must've bought a new one, but there were letters burnt into the black plastic that said the council owned the radio, that it belonged to the city, that it belonged to the state, but I burned off the letters with a lighter and got the plastic to melt, got it to go completely gooey and sticky, and then I smoothed out those state-owned letters, and then I said I'd found it, that someone had thrown it away cos they'd probably put it on the hob or something, and I don't know if she believed me, but it could have been true, and then we had that radio in the kitchen, on the windowsill, for years, and it worked well, and I used it, that lovely black radio with red detailing, and burned-in letters that were no longer visible, no longer applicable, I used it a lot, I took it into my room in the evening and listened to the radio, listened to the radio programmes, they came from another world, they came from the other side of the sea, the other side of the giant ocean I'd learned that some children could cross, in little dinghies, in little wooden boats, made from reclining chairs and tables, and sails made of sheets and towels, and I closed my eyes and listened, closed my eyes and saw other worlds and other lives before me, others' lives, better lives, while I listened to programmes with names like *Eldorado* and *Inferno* and *Soul Corner* and *Slammer*, and I listened and thought and listened and soon learned to recognise the sounds I liked,

the ones that sounded different to the ones I was used
to, but also words and sounds that in different ways
related to the life I recognised, the pain and the rage and
the shame and the hate and the madness, like when I, at
Eleonora's place, got to hear Godflesh and Slayer for the
first time, and at that point, as I listened, it was like my
life got better, like it really, properly, got noticeably better
just cos some guy had stood there yelling in a studio, as
though my life became another as I lay there with my
ear to the state's little loudspeaker, when I recorded the
songs or whole radio programmes, so I could listen again
and again, but the whole time I knew it was stolen, that
I'd nicked that shit, and it was the same with the lamps
and the candlesticks and picture frames, every time we
used them we'd feel ashamed, and we knew that as we
stood there in the dumpster and looked around us, a bag
of clothes was ripped open and we looked at them, looked
to see if they could be worn, that they fit, that they were
intact, that they didn't stink of piss or shit or puke or
mould, and the fear of being discovered was double, on
one hand residents, janitors, cops and shit, on the other
people we knew, our fear of being branded *dumpster divers*,
which was what we were, the terror of being branded
down-and-outs, which we were, social cases, yeah, like
the poor fucking dumpster-diving family we really were,
that was precisely what we were, penniless social cases
who rummaged through dumpsters after nice things to
have in our home, nice things to wear on our bodies, and
we continued to be dumpster divers till Securitas started
patrolling that shit and the people who threw out things
that worked started locking up their rubbish, cos it was
theirs, cos they'd learned the art of *telling yours from mine*,

as the pigs would put it, and they were proper, sturdy locks, made from toughened steel and that dot that meant they were difficult to open, that you couldn't pick with those kiddies' picklocks I carried with me, picklocks I made from those little key-type things you open sardine tins with, cans of processed ham or whatever it's called, help me, food, keys, picks, ham, pigs, cops, cans, aluminium, shit bro, everything's spinning, I mean, wait a bit, good people, forgive me, my head's spinning, I can't talk properly, I've got something in my mouth, I've got a mouth full of food, of blood and pig, and Danne's bloody nose under my fist and my stranglehold, and his eyes, his piggy eyes, staring and showing he took back what he'd said, what he'd said about us being dumpster divers and dropouts, which we were, but I threatened him anyway, knocked him down and sat on him and threw a few punches, held my hand round his throat, and his eyes opened wide like he was a little pig, or a little calf, a tasty little morsel of meat, and there was some other pig I did in when he said Dad was an alkie, which he was, but he still got a fat thump on the kisser and then he kept quiet about it, it's not a thing I wanna be reminded of the whole time, right, little piggy, not even I wanna talk about it, not even now, I mean, everyone already knows everything, everyone out here's already heard it, I don't know, Cody, I don't know why I'm going over this again, over and over again, this mess, over and over again, this miserable shit, this murderously boring dirge, I don't know Cody, I don't fucking know, I'd rather give it a miss, be someone else, have a different mouth, without bloody pigs in, without that taste, without these words, it's so meaningless and boring and I don't even care, and why should I care, who cares, shit, Cody, forgive me, I don't know, it's against my will, believe me, that much I know, it's *not* my intention, it's *against* my will, *against* my intentions, as I said, yeah, the desire to shut my mouth is greater, always, stronger, cos the sounds that come out of my open mouth have nothing to do with anything, nothing real, nothing more than guts full of shit and bloody pigs, and I know it, and I'm longing for peace, to get away from the sound of my own voice, get out of my own shit-streaked pig's head, believe me, bro, the impulse to shut my mouth once and for all is strong, but it's like I can't do it, I can't, it just happens, it opens like a well-fucked anus and all that shit leaks out, and then suddenly my mouth is full of it again, of names and places, of events and movements, of memories and images, I have a mouth full of ugly memories and ugly words, I can feel it, how I stand there with my mouth open, open like an idiot, and my head is full of ugly blood, my eyes, I really can see it the whole time, I have waking dreams about it in the day and I dream about it at night, I have a brain full of it, Cody, my whole mouth is full of blood, my mouth is full of earth, my mouth is full of names, my mouth is full of you, my mouth is full of your ears and your mouth, my mouth is full of your sealed lips, which are hard as they press against my lips, almost like a cock, a cock with teeth, my mouth is full of your face and I'm eating earth full of worms that tie themselves in knots in my throat, earth and gravel that scrapes against my palate, my cheeks sink in, my mouth is twisted by teeth biting and consuming it, my mouth is full of figures and letters and words and images I looked at in those papers I went round trying to sell, and those flyers I handed out, when I was trying to be an honest little boy, an honourable little saint with no need to care about the pig's blood and the rubbish and the earth, when I worked, when I believed, without understanding that that was what I believed, or that I believed anything at all, since I couldn't think, since everything was so self-evident, so clear, a given, yeah, precisely, a given, but I thought, you know, that there was some simple way out of all the shit I'd ended up in, that we'd all ended up in, landed in, fallen down into, been thrown into, been forced, pressed, screwed down into, and I went round, I was twelve, and I went round, handing out flyers, I don't remember what the flyers were for, none of that exists any more, none of the companies or the shops or the logos or the subs, none of those words and images, nothing at all of all that stuff I looked at and read again and again, the stuff that used to bother me so much, that filled me and shaped me, nothing, not one word, not one image, not one single letter or colour remains, just the feeling of being bothered, the smell of the paper and how it felt to touch the paper, just my filled and formed mind and body, the same mind and the same body that went round selling papers sweating like a little geek, and it took a while before I realised it was totally meaningless, that it was better to sell hash or at least moonshine to the alkies, cos you earned next to nothing for the legal stuff, not a fucking thing, and there I was going around like an idiot with these papers over my left arm, ringing on doors, saying: hello, or good afternoon, or good evening, would you like to buy the *Evening Post* today, the same fucking *Evening Post* that had interviewed the older guys who were now even older and into darker things and wouldn't let themselves be interviewed by some *lófasz* from the paper and definitely not photo-graphed by some *malakas* photographer; if they were caught on camera, it would most likely be CCTV picking out their dark silhouettes as they tried to break into a post office or the like, the kind of thing that still existed out there back then, before they gave up on it all and closed and shut all that shit down, so that nothing became even less, that is, even more nothing, but there I was anyway, going out to sell this bloody piss, and I said hello, or good afternoon or good evening or just: an *Evening Post* today? and I think they were six krona each, and then one krona went to me, I think, and I'm not joking, one lousy coin, man, and I wasn't exactly chasing big bucks like the kids do these days, boast about these days, but the gold ten-krona coin was new and sometimes I got one and they said: keep the change, you know. I realised pretty soon it was pointless to go around like a fucking beggar for a krona here and a krona there, it was really hard to sell that jumped-up shit posing as eloquence and poetry too, but you know how it is, one day someone stole a paper, cos they used to dump them, in bundles, by the cycle path, and you were meant to ring in and report them stolen, then they took it off what you owed, so I told them three had gone and then I sold them and made 100 per cent on them, of course, and then I did it more and more, and of course everyone knew only thieves and immigrants lived out there, and so it was sorted, more for my pocket, 100 per cent, right, but you know, they realised pretty soon that something wasn't right, and I got the sack, I think, somehow or other, and I remember sitting there anxiously by the phone, our first one with button tones or whatever you call it, plasticky with a tangled wire, you had to ring in and punch and punch and it beeped and beeped, and the whole time I was wondering what they were gonna do if they caught up with me, but nothing happened, I just got the sack, had to start from scratch with zero cash in my pocket. Then I delivered flyers, you had to sit there night after night, doing the inserts, my mum and sister helped sometimes, then up and down the stairwells like an idiot, fingers shredded by paper cuts and those damn letter boxes ripping up my cuticles every time I put my hand through, didn't get paid shit either, but at least I had music in my ears, music I'd recorded from the radio, with the help of the thieved radio, the lovely black thieved radio with the red detailing, and that music made me, sometimes, dumb as I was, think it was totally fine, like it wouldn't have been better to sit in some quiet place, or go walk somewhere, listening to that same music, instead of running up and down those stairs like a fucking idiot, and that wasn't even the worst part, far from it, no, the worst part was doing the inserts, there were maybe ten different flyers, and they all had to go inside the largest one, and you know, it's Friday and you're sitting there doing the inserts in front of the TV like an idiot, bunking off school to get through that shit, but anyway, it was only mother-tongue study sessions and we never did a thing in those anyway, so now I had to sit there doing inserts in front of the fucking TV, Mum's watching *Oprah*, Mum's watching *The Bold and the Beautiful*, or QVC is rolling, you know, headphones on, then Saturday evening and we're stuffing flyers in front of the fucking TV, I'm thinking I'm gonna flip, I swear, Mum, any time now, need to take a walk to the fast-food stand, meet Rodde, smoke a straight, calm myself down, and at that point I hadn't even started thinking about the older guys with their Mercs and BMWs and their deals and their runners, still, Saturday and Sunday always came round and it was time to head out and do the delivery, up and down like an idiot, totally owned like some little cunt, some piss-poor little prick, like air, know what I mean Cody? It's these things I have in my mouth, and since I'm talking about jobs there's one thing I've just got to say, Cody, are you listening? There was this time I was gonna park down here on the street. I found a gap, pulled up gently alongside a shining-white Audi and reversed in smoothly, in a single move-ment, and just as I was opening the door, about to get out of the car, I saw something, something big driving up behind me. So I stayed sitting there, pulled the door back to halfway and looked up at the passenger seat of this minibus. And I saw a pale man in his twenties froth-ing at the mouth and laughing. It took two seconds for the minibus to drive by, but the image of this man's sort of delirious gaze, his cheeks and chin bubbling with saliva, it stayed with me and pushed me down into my seat, as two memories popped up simultaneously. They were memories from two different times in my life, now brought together, placed next to each other, or like a double exposure in that one moment. In one of the mem-ories I'm sitting in the passenger seat of a small truck. The man driving is the boss of a company that imports and sells cut flowers to florists. I work at his warehouse along with two Poles and an Albanian. We unpack flowers, roses from Kenya for instance, that come packed in large boxes, we repack them in bunches, five at a time or ten at a time, or in special bouquets, in the run-up to the

Midsummer holiday, for instance, and put them in buckets with water and little paper labels with flower feed or whatever. It's cash in hand, the work's monotonous and there's almost always overtime, since the boss is a workaholic, as they say, and demands everyone works as much as he does. The difference is we're standing up all day, at the same workbench, apart from thirty minutes' lunch and short fag breaks, while he's sitting at his desk, positioned so he can see everything we're doing, for long periods, and at regular intervals he disappears off to do some shit or other. Helge or Stig – or something like that, I can't remember – is capricious, sometimes friendly and generous, sometimes sullen and complaining. You have to ask permission to use the toilet. So one day we're sitting in this little truck Helgestig has hired from like Hertz or something to drive some stuff to the old folks' home his dad's just moved to. He asked me and I agreed, on condition of payment, naturally, the same pay as I got at the warehouse. We're sitting in the truck and he starts chatting about young immigrant men with flash cars. That he can guarantee, with very few exceptions, that they're criminals. I'm dumbfounded, unsure how far what he's saying is aimed at me. Not that I have a car, I didn't even have a licence at that point, but you know, I've only been working for him for a couple of weeks and I've already realised he's a bastard. Like a lot of times already, I just want to ask him to shut his mouth, which I can't do of course, cos I need the money to pay for a flat I'm renting over the summer (after that I don't know where I'll be living). Then we drive past a minor accident, a car has gone into the back of another at a red light. Helgesigge says: oh dear, little darkie. If you've gone into the back of someone it's nobody's fault but your own, however much your little introspections succeed. Yeah, that was one of the memories. That: *your little introspections succeed.* I don't know why it just occurred to me now. The other memory is me coming home from this job washing dishes at a restaurant, it's late, and I have that taste in my mouth and I've found my roommate Erik lying on the sofa in front of the TV. He's totally gone on ket and started foaming at the mouth; it's running from the corners of his mouth down onto his skinny, hairless chest where it's collecting in a little pool. For a little while I'm genuinely scared and try to assess if it's a serious overdose. On the coffee table is a piece of paper with a big heap of the stuff. Erik's recently started selling K to stay solvent, so to speak, money-wise, since losing his job. He buys it by the bottle, in liquid form, and cooks it down in a Teflon pan. We talk for a bit, I tell him not to take any more today, put away the wrap and throw him a tissue. He tries to wipe his mouth and chest, but just spreads the saliva out. I sit with him for a while to see how he's doing. It seems OK, but what the hell do I know. I smoke a joint and tease him a bit. We've discussed this before, the dangers of suddenly finding yourself with large quantities of powder. You'll end up like Scarface, I said. Then we called him Tony Montana for a while. Erik was totally convinced it would be easy to resist the temptation to snort it all, cos he needed the money. How fucking dumb are you? I say. He smiles blissfully. Then I've had enough and leave him, almost hoping he chokes on his own vomit, go into the bedroom and lie on my bed and listen to something, maybe Drexciya or *Philophobia*, or *Things Fall Apart* or like DJ Krush and Toshinori Kondo, the *Ki-Oku* record I guess, I was pretty obsessed with it at that point (I remember when my dad heard a track from that record, he laughed scornfully and was like: who's that playing at being Miles Davis?). Or maybe it was *Kakusei*, that had that track 'Crimson' I think it's called, with the Harold Budd sample, from 'Bismillahi 'Rrahmani 'Rrahim', but I don't know what that means, and I didn't know that Krush, or Hideaki Ishi as he's really called, was a petty criminal in his youth, was even a member of the Yakuza, but I often used to listen to 'Survival of the Fittest' on the way to work, and I don't know what to say about that kind of social Darwinism, like in Mobb Deep's track of the same name, or in 'Shook Ones part II': *Rock you in your face, stab your brain with your nose bone*, but CL Smooth is so sick in that, or that one with Tragedy Khadafi, aka Intelligent Hoodlum, you know (which makes me think of Killer Mike and his: *I'm a young G, I'm a EV, Educated Villain*, and *I'm a book reader, I'm a gang leader*), who says in a video clip: *To me it ain't no love out there, y'know what I'm sayin' . . . everybody . . . everybody just like robots right now . . . like zombies . . . ain't no love out there . . . I think the future gonna be a scary thing . . . like y'know . . . gotta get ready for it . . . y'know what I'm sayin' . . . if you ain't tryin' to get ready for it, then just get high and get bent . . . y'know what I'm sayin' . . . and let it come or go or whatever . . . that's my fuckin' philosophy on the future . . .* and that was more or less what we did, got high and got bent, weren't really ready for anything at all, right Cody, right man, and yeah, worked and worked of course, worked and thieved a bit sometimes, or quite a lot really, shotted a bit, not a lot but a bit, right, and slept a lot too, slept whole days sometimes, found it really hard to get up in the morning, I didn't really get up before one, and I almost always had massive anxiety in the morning, which meant a spliff with my coffee and it eased a little, then you could just lie there, lazing in bed a while, read a magazine, a book, snooze, watch some porn, wank, fall asleep again, chill, and get into weird states, hypnagogic states, as they call it, till you felt like a failure and just wanted to die and fall asleep again, but sometimes you came up with really great solutions to all kinds of problems, mostly how we'd get on in life and stop having to work, and stealing and sleeping and shit, but it carried on instead and there was more and more of it, that's what it felt like anyway, time just passed and I just wasted it, I wasn't stupid, I knew that, thought about it all the time, I mean if you listen to that survival-of-the-fittest shit at the same time as being totally lost, a layabout, I mean you feel it the whole time, you're no gangster, you're not king of anything, you're no knight, no ninja, no survivor, you know, and I thought about it all the time, as I was standing waiting for the bus, going one way or the other, when I was waiting for a shift to finish, when I was working ten hours straight on a building site for loose change that took an evening to drink and smoke away, but you knew the only thing worse was no job at all, no cash at all, so yeah, you worked and I still have that taste in my mouth, of dust, coffee, fags, a nagging boss, the taste of sweaty, reused face masks, the taste of work, the taste of the same thing all the time, again and again, back and forth, round and round, that's what I have in my mouth, several metres of guts and shit and I don't wanna talk about it, I don't even wanna think about it, you get me, I don't wanna have it in me, in my throat, on my tongue, in my mouth, but every time I open my mouth, out it runs, what can I do, I open my mouth to say something completely different or just to breathe and this shit runs out, all these things run out, everything just pours out, symbols, figures, letters, numbers, images, films, stories, tragic, funny, like the one about two boys out walking one day, they'd left their homes and made their way into the big wide world, as they say, and then this happened. It was Saturday. They were sitting on a bench by a kiosk. Behind them were a school, a few bushes, a roundabout and some houses and a car park with cars parked in shining rows. The boys had a fag and shared a can of Coke and a Snickers and talked vaguely about things they were interested in, about life, about music, about some album covers, about skulls and a few other things. Then a car pulled up. A man got out and asked if they wanted work. Employment, he said. Earn a little money, he said. They asked what they'd be doing. Handing out flyers, he said. For his building firm. Go around the wealthy neighbourhoods and stuff a few flyers through letterboxes. They asked how much they'd get. Five hundred. To share. Course we will, they said. That's a lot of money, they thought. They got in the car. He drove them to the wealthy neighbourhood. They got a stack each. Took a side each and put them in the letter boxes as he drove along behind them, crept along slowly behind them. After a while they'd run out of flyers. Oops, Builder Man said. We'll have to get some more, it looks as though I've left them at home. It'll only take a minute, he said. After that you'll get your cash. OK, but it better be quick, the boys said. And then we'll have the cash. They drove out to his house. You can smoke in the car if you want, he said. Then they arrived. It was a big house by a field.

He went in to get the bundles. They stayed in the car. Smoked. Looked through the glove box for something to steal. There was nothing, just receipts and pens and bad music on cassette. Builder Man came back with two boxes. He put them in the boot and sat in the driver's seat. Right, he said. Let's be off. Then he said something about the car. He asked if they could drive. They said no. Do you want to have a go? he said. Of course, they thought. Can we try it? they said. Yes, he said. It's not hard. It takes a while to learn the pedals, but I can do them. You can sit in front of me, he said. You do the steering wheel, I'll do the pedals. They said yes. First one. There wasn't much space up there. Can you move the seat back further, the boy said. That's as far as it goes, Builder Man said. So he ended up sitting on Builder Man's knee. OK, drive then, the boy said. He drove slowly. The boy held the wheel with both hands. At ten to two. He laughed. Looked behind him at the other boy. Watch the road, he laughed. Builder Man did the pedals and held the bottom of the steering wheel with one hand. At six. He sped up. He steered a little, down there at six, occasionally letting go of the wheel and letting his hand rest there. By the boy's cock. The other hand rested on the boy's thigh. He sped up a little more. The boy watched the road. The lines and the ditch. He swerved a little from left to right. The boy in the back seat laughed. They talked about driving. The car was moving quickly along the empty road. Builder Man stroked his hand back and forth across the boy's cock. That was what he did. And sometimes he moved the boy's whole body so it pressed against Builder Man's hip, against his cock. The boy felt this with some kind of vague surprise, Builder Man's hand stroking his cock, back and forth, and up and down. It wasn't fear the boy felt, more a diffuse discomfort. He watched the road and thought about how he was driving the car. Or was he really? he thought. Sometimes Builder Man let go of the wheel, resting both hands in the boy's lap, on the insides of the boy's thighs. Shifted the boy's body again. Picked him up and released him. Stroked his hand across his cock again. It wasn't fear. It was uncertainty. About whether he was just imagining it all. About whether he was maybe enjoying it. The car moved forward. Ditches, fields, solitary houses. Hands on the boy. That was all. Then they stopped. Now it was the other boy's turn. The first said nothing. They talked about driving. Same thing with the other boy. They drove. They didn't know where they were. An hour had passed, more, since they'd picked up the boxes. You know what, Builder Man said. It's late. You can do the rest next time. You can have the money. Asked if he should drive them home. Supposed it was getting dark. They told him where they lived and that he could drive them. They got a 500-krona note. His number. For when they wanted some more work. You never know when you might need a little money, he laughed, and if there's one thing that's true in this world, it's that you always need a few coins in your pocket, so the dogs won't piss on you, and that was what I was thinking about as I stood there, feeling dirty and weak under the tall street lights by the turning area, in the night, by the car park, just before the big meadow and the fields began, by the turning area where he'd dropped us off a few hours earlier, under the street light, in the ochre light, and I exhaled smoke and the cloud floated up towards the light and got bigger and bigger until it was completely impossible that that cloud had just been inside my body, in my lungs, then come up through my throat and out through my mouth, up towards the light, and I guess it's that I have in my mouth now, that lesson, that truth, that if you have no money you can't buy nothing, but if you've got a little cash, a little paper, a little green, a few p's, well then, you can suddenly get anything you want, you get me, man? You get what I mean, Cody? You hear what I'm saying? I thought as the guitarist looked at me and I strained my face in an attempt to focus on his face, on his eyes. But y'know, I really like that, he said, that O'Carolan didn't bid farewell to life, to the world, but to music. I took a deep breath and heard the composer say: yeah, but what does it mean, that he didn't think he'd be able to experience music after his death? I tried to understand what they were talking about and noticed the canal was full of rubbish, bobbing about on the surface: plastic bags, bottles, a metre-long metal stick glistening. Two kayaks came gliding along on the water. Or is it about life continuing, after death, so to speak? Well, I don't really know what he meant, said the guitarist, or how he imagined the whole thing. No, I said, and I was about to say something about Scelsi's string quartet but the words got stuck in my throat again, and after a while the composer said that thing about mathematics is interesting, and she said something about *sacred geometry*, but I didn't hear cos I was thinking about Soot again, I was still thinking about Soot, and about that place I was intended for, that I'd escaped, on the roundabout, in the bus, that motion that went on and on, within and without me.

The whole morning, while practising a Scelsi piece – his fourth String Quartet, to be precise – I kept glancing at the wax-plant flowers that had opened during the night. The white and pink blossoms hung in clusters and looked like tiny little eyes watching over me: a little audience from another species, I thought afterwards, in the afternoon, as I stood by the canal, by the gravel path between the police station and the water, and waited for the guitarist and the composer. I was meant to be going to Copenhagen with them to hear a concert by the German organist Christoph Maria Moosmann at the cathedral, Vor Frue Kirke. Moosmann would be playing pieces by Pärt and Cage, and *In Nomine Lucis*, by Scelsi himself, a piece that sounded absolutely magnificent on a church organ, I knew that from experience because I'd heard Kevin Bowyer play it, it was quite clearly in the same class – as I asserted then, at least – as the best works for organ by Messiaen and Bach. But that morning I didn't give any of that a thought. As with all successful rehearsals, I was completely reset, emptied of words and concepts, free of thoughts, memories and desires, and yet in the grip of some centripetal motion, on the way to something significant. I looked at the sheet music in front of me and breathed. My ribcage, my lungs and my arms were moving. My elbows were moving, and my fingers. Sound became flesh, body. I closed my eyes and was no longer myself. Now we were approaching the central station, and the guitarist said something about the time, presumably because he'd caught sight of the clock up on the tower. He said we had plenty of time after all, assuming the train wasn't delayed, and I said it was probably going to be fine, at the same time as I thought I should ask the composer to repeat what she'd said a minute ago, about geometry, and that I wanted to tell them about Scelsi's Fourth String Quartet, which, I was pretty sure, neither the guitarist nor the composer were that closely acquainted with. The most interesting thing, I wanted to say, was, aside from many things I'd like to come back to (for instance its scordatura and the relationship with the golden ratio), the notation. The piece was written in such a way that every string had its own stave in the score, as though it were composed for sixteen instruments, rather than the quartet's four, and as though I, normally responsible for one instrument, with a relatively broad register, was now playing four instruments, which independently, and viewed as instruments, were poorer in terms of expression and tone, but which, in some way, and this was what I wanted to discuss with the guitarist and the composer, together succeeded in constituting something that was *different*, that was *more* than a cello, and which, assuming the same was the case for the quartet's other instruments, meant we were something other than a string quartet. But what? And why? And how did that fit with the character of the piece, that striving, ascending, descending, trembling, like a tug-of-war between weight and levity, between descent and ascent? Playing it felt, on the whole, like falling upwards. Does that sound feasible? I wanted to ask the composer. What was it she'd said about geometry? I hadn't been able to make out her words, I'd been thinking about Soot instead, as though he was standing before me, swaying just above me, in a kind of formless guise, unfathomable, an invisible light, and hearing him say, voicelessly, yes, soundlessly: so I don't know, Cody. *Why?* A soldier dies, gets shot down. Nothing so strange about that, is there? That's what they do, soldiers. They die, fall, drop their guns, someone captures them in that moment, on film, mid-fall, *falling*, in the air. Someone takes a picture, it gets turned into a banner, makes its way around the world. Then we're sitting there, a bunch of years later, under that picture, and Denzo digs out a bit of standard and roasts the tobacco and you start thinking, finally a little peace and quiet, finally a little *respite*, as they say, finally *respectus, refugium, sanctum*, the kind of stuff the coconuts come out with, and you know my dad told me this is *paradise*, and thirty years later he'd acknowledge that the whole thing had been a bluff, a lie, that he regretted the whole move, the emigration, as he put it, the *emigration*, cos, you know, he was never an immigrant in his own mind, no fucking immigrant, he was an emigrant, man, an exile, brah, and he said he regretted all his thirty years in exile, he was sorry for it, you know, wanted to ask forgiveness for everything then, when it was already too late, but you know, we were just sitting there under the banner with the dying soldier and we carefully sent round the bong, and I puked later, again, as per, with Denzo, that was his name, he was the one, but why? we laughed, do you remember? Metallica's double basses, some cripple in a video, ah, I don't know, there's no justice, *I cannot live, I cannot die, trapped in myself, absolute horror*, and Mum watching *Oprah*, watching *The Bold and the Beautiful*, and you know, did you know Olga moved back to Kazakhstan, but you know, soon she fell over the Russian border, started streetwalking, as they say, in Novokuznetsk, started shooting up speed and horse, I know this cos I spoke to her two months after she'd gone, but then it went quiet and there were rumours she'd started using krokodil, and in that case they'll be burying the rest of her worn-out body soon enough, but I mean, I swear, you know that guy Anden, the guy who was playing the big man in the yard, when we fought I called him a nigger and he called me a cunt or a queer, that's what we used to say when we were kids, but it's not him, and it's not Denzo, not him, I think he's alive, and it's not Niko, we called him Niko, his name was Niklas, and he died, he died – what – ten, is it already ten years ago, he died in front of the TV, his mum found him, did you know that? Died in front of the TV, heart stopped beating or something, stopped breathing, suffocated by his own vomit, I don't know what happens when you shoot too much horse, but his mum found him in front of the TV, dead, overdose, and I always think about TV static and about his mum coming into the room and seeing her son is dead, this guy, you know, who I used to play with once, and I mean you can ask yourself *why* here, you get me, he was no soldier, or OK, maybe he was, I mean, what is a war? I guess it's about finding the biggest gang. Arben preferred to head over to Kosovo rather than stay here with his anxiety, if you remember, and at the time we thought how the fuck can he do that? But today it's totally obvious, why shouldn't he go over there? And today they go to new places, where the biggest gangs are, the ones open to them in any case, I mean they could hardly join the cops or the military, too late for that, but I don't know, what do I know, this has nothing to do with Niko either, he was just a regular junkie, and I don't know why I thought of the TV static either, if he was watching TV it was probably playing, just cos he died it didn't make the TV stop, I mean everything goes on I guess, life goes on, the TV goes on, the ads go on, the news goes on, the series, the films, the chat shows, the comedies, the thrillers, the tear-jerkers, the cop shows, and at some point his mum came into the room and saw her kid as a corpse, and so she lifted up his head, and you know how heavy and cold a dead head is, it weighs a fucking ton, mate, and she hit him over the head and over the chest and jerked her kid about, pulling at this corpse, trying and failing to shake some life into her kid, his life was gone, it was over, she'd seen it come and go, once he didn't exist, then he did, and now he didn't again, just as all other life was continuing, and that bit is hard to get your head around, I know that, but sorry, Cody, forgive me, I don't wanna talk about this, it's getting ridiculous, I'm embarrassed, I don't wanna think about it, I don't wanna paint these pictures, cos I know how people react when they see them, like we did when we sat in Denzo's room at the home, under that poster, like *why?*, you just have to take the piss out of it, you have to laugh at it, you have to be like, *and?*, a junkie dies, a soldier dies, a thieving immigrant gets a bullet behind the ear, a bullet in the stomach, a bullet through the heart, and so what? Believe me, I don't want to, if it was my choice I'd keep my mouth shut and glide on by, but I can't cos my eyes are swimming in it, and it's roaring in my ears and my whole mouth is really full of it, of his body, his child-body, of the fact that we were children, that we were playing, as it used to be known when we were little, that we walked along talking, just as usual, as children do, walked, talked, thought, played, and then the static, then the cold heavy head, and his mum's gaze, but I don't know what it was, his dad died of an overdose too I think. Niko I call him, he lived in Möllevången, we went back to his place, watched some Bruce Lee film, clips from old ninja films, he always talked so much shit, *mything*, that's what we used to call it, got *hossi*, as we put it, lied and boasted and manipulated, always had to show he was the biggest and the strongest, even as a kid, yeah, I think his dad overdosed too, earlier, when Niko was little, but I don't know, he rang me too, later, when we were older, a year or so before he died, and it's like I said, you laugh at things like that, at people like him, I can't remember what he wanted, just that I didn't want to talk to him, he was so irritating, such a *hossi*, he lied and it was obvious, no self-awareness, no respect, too much attitude, so it's not him, he's already dead and buried, and I wasn't there, I don't know, maybe someone from the family, what could he have been, around twenty, still a brother in some ways, like you, right *bratku*, right Cody, brah, tell me to shut my mouth now, I wanna shut my mouth, seal up this hole, make it disappear, fade away, into the haze, as they say, another haze, but I see it the whole time, my eyes are like swimming in it, my eyes are like made of it, it's inside my head, like a filter, like a note on an organ, a membrane, I don't know, I really don't know who's lying in the coffin, in the cremation chamber, but it's not Caro, in any case, cos she did her months, got focused, got a new life and left Vlad and his dirty shotter's life, and it's not Saladin and co, they're still alive, still getting vex, yeah, but I've seen them myself, and not Ronny, Nenad or Said, cos they're all living totally normal *suedi*-lives, with pensions and summer houses, and it's not Tindra, as she used to call herself, cos she's still alive too, she might have done herself in, yeah, but she's still living, and to be honest, that's probably what you'd say about me, right Cody? Isn't that how it sounds when you open your mouth and talk about your friend, your comrade, your bro, you say no, it's not Soot this time, he's still alive, they say, he's alive, homeless and half-psychotic most of the time, but he's alive, and a load of crap about cherry orchards blah blah blah, I'm gonna flip out soon, you're always talking so much fucking shit. Isn't that how it is, Cody? Isn't that what you say? Not Soot, no, no he's alive, he's worn out but he's alive, and you know when we were little we kissed to test it out, like queers, yeah, precisely, when we were little we drank rum and smoked hash, smoked kush, smoking weed, like brothers, snogging like *blutte* batty boys, not a word about it to anyone, keeping it on the down-low, batty bros, is that what you say, man, tongue brothers, and hung out with hot Turkish girls outside the pool, I remember that, one was called Ayşen, the other I don't know, something beginning with T I think, but back then we were brothers, right, *bratku*, punks and hard rockers, brats, kids, snotty little kids with fags and hash and marker pens in bumbags, we ran around at night with butterfly knives and stilettos, Reeperbahn, Altona,

Karoviertel, right *digga*, broke into places, stole, when
we were little, went to gigs at Die Fabrik, Docks, Große
Freiheit, Markthalle, Störtebeker, saw Fugazi, Cypress
Hill, Sick of It All, Strife, Unsane, moshed stoned in sweat,
blood and spit, adrenalin-racing little animals, that whole
white-trash thing, fucking hostile, bumfluffed little boys,
steeped in that American shit, and we watched the films,
looked at the records, slammed here and pogoed there,
just another victim, kid, with our bloody noses clotting, but
whose blood is that, *kid*? Isn't that what you say, Cody?
Sat up late at night watching video after video, Suicidal
Tendencies and *War Inside My Head*, but also Psí Vojáci,
the dog soldiers, and later on their song about razor blades
too, razor blades on the body, razor blades in the body,
and our dads who'd both cut their arms, such brothers,
and his mum who said she'd heard it was the sweetest
thing, when your body drains of blood, when the life runs
out, better than the best drugs, better than crack, better
than a speedball, but what happens? we asked, it's like
you rise and sink at the same time, and we creased up,
we laughed, drank powdered ice tea and went on little
trips to the sea, I remember that guy who'd never seen
the sea, went to Heligoland, stole little bottles of spirits
in the shop and hid in a cubbyhole under a stairwell on
the ferry, down it, neck it, creasing up like idiots, Sweden
doesn't exist, Denmark's going under, Germany we love
you, Yugoslavia's burning, Europe is the future, the Eastern
European kids fuck themselves in the arse with turquoise
double-enders, their tender, oozing dreams flowing like
pure shit, what's happening, man, how hard can life be,
really, if we're honest, and how tender is it to die by your
own hand, just how, how focused do you have to be, yeah,

yeah, it was screwed up, and being screwed up was something to aspire to, so we fucked off down to Bambule, floated about between the scabby caravans, the mud, the planks, the rubbish, the smoke and the fires in big rusty barrels, in shopping trolleys, the rags, fighting words, flags, it was anarchy for idiots, we said to each other, even we, we said, children, have started reading Bakunin and Goldman, but those guys and their girlfriends are pure 100 per cent idiots, we said to each other, cracking up, they're retarded kids, we said to each other, and in the dark we could make out a mannequin with no legs, covered with tags and stickers, we knocked on the door to the dealer's house, the fat anarchist pig was lying there watching a film, some imbecile American film, his expensive fucking bike hung on the wall, clean and lovely in that shithole, a block of a couple of ounces or more on the little coffee table. *Was geht, digga?* we said. What you want, he said, the ugly anarchist, and we had twenty DM so Soot said we wanted a twenty's-worth, and the big freedom-loving anarchist with tattoos that must have cost half a year's salary on his body, he laughed at us. A twenty? Motherfucking kids, I can't even be fucked getting up for a twenty, and we stood there, thinking and gauging, and then we went up to the bed and smashed a beer bottle over the head of that revolutionary little anarchist bitch, took out a knife, and Soot just held it two inches in front of that pale anarchist head, and we stood like that for a while, nothing happening except for my heart beating fucking hard, and the big man rebel anarchist went on mocking, saying shit like we should go to hell and fuck our mothers and we were snotty kids, but that was cool cos we could see he was afraid and in the end he got off his fat arse and cut what must have been a quarter and didn't even dare do anything when he didn't get our twenty, though we still didn't risk walking off with the whole block, just said that's how it goes, you lazy cunt, and walked out and spat at his door and then ran as fast as we could, past all the caravans, and all the scabby punks with their Bad Religion shirts and rich parents in Bavaria, and then we couldn't go back and buy from there for several months, but it made no difference cos we found a new source and so on and so forth, is that how it is, Cody, and you say actually that's true, we'd started reading, and we'd started talking about books, yeah, it's true, me and Soot, when we were younger we talked about Kafka, with our bumfluff-stoner vocab, about *Metamorphosis*, we smoked bongs and I puked all over his room, we had to cut off a bit of his carpet after that, and we hung out in the squat on Laeiszstrasse, or wherever the hell it was, and at some mate of Soot's who played Snoop the whole fucking time and I hugged the toilet bowl and puked and puked and puked till thick yellow bile came up and my stomach kept churning but nothing else would come up and Snoop was Snoop Doggy Dogg in the background, and all that shit, it's so boring, but that's the kind of thing you say, right Cody? Isn't it? But I don't know, it's not like we didn't try, Cody, right, I mean, I really did go into that last interview with the best of intentions, as they say, to get on that course, to get that job as a truck driver, and they asked a load of questions and I replied and I said those words, born in Prague, and I knew they'd light up and say, oh, it's beautiful there, and I knew those mental images had captions like Charles Bridge, Rococo and Art Nouveau, and believe me, Cody, believe me, I know all about that stuff, I know all about Art Nouveau and all that shit, or at least as much as them, I've done graffiti my whole life, right, and I've flicked through those books too, I've sat in the library, I'm not thick, I know where I come from, and I know what they saw, they saw the castle lit up at night, they saw gilded spires stretching up into the sky, stretching up, everything stretching up, like Mucha's foliage, more and more slender, like Schiele's bodies, everything wanting to lift and shine up into the heavens, into something beautiful and almost divine, but of course retaining its weight and its trademarked Kafkaesque despair, and perhaps they'd read Hrabal too and now they saw some charming drunk stumbling home over the Staromák cobbles, mumbling secrets to the strains of some trademarked dissident jazz, just as charmingly dilapidated, or some fucking gypsy fiddler or something, but you know, I'm not from there, I wanted to say, that's got nothing to do with me, you know, up there, in there, that's where the decision-makers live, I wanted to say, but didn't, you know, I come from places decision-makers never come from, I didn't say either, I come from Háje, I didn't say, but should have, that's in Prague too, go home and google it, I come from Jižní Město, from Jížák, from the final station, always the final station, go home and google that instead, I didn't say but should have, don't think Bedřich Smetana, think Peneři Strýčka Homeboye, you get me, don't even think Plastic People or DG 307, or some shit like that from the seventies when our grandparents worked their arses off, kept their mouths shut and our mums toiled away at home and searched for our fathers who'd gone hiding in bars behind beards and long hair and antisocial countercultures, think more Chaozz and Prago Union, Naše Věc and DeFuckTo, you know, just smoking weed and no future, you get me, but you don't, I didn't say, instead I just said yes, it's beautiful, and it was true in a way, cos it is, it is beautiful, in its way, even if it's ugly, if you see what I mean, but you don't, or, I dunno, maybe not beautiful, I dunno if it's really that beautiful, the buildings I mean, the streets, and the greenery and shit, but I mean the other stuff, I like coming out onto the street early on an autumn morning, or that there's at least something small, a small, small part of that, though of course you're stressed out cos you're on your way to some shitty job, if you're lucky, on your way to being screwed in the head as per. But still, there's something small, a part of it, something I quite like when I'm walking along in the morning, perhaps it's a little chilly, kind of misty, or dewy, or whatever, it's early autumn, mid-September, the leaves have begun to settle on the ground and I come out onto the street and immediately see a bunch of scaffolders banging their metal pipes and wooden planks about, their chat, wet and Polish or sharp and Lithuanian, and then some toothless copper thief comes cycling along with his toolbox and his little solar-powered radio, his body broken by addiction, but those hands holding the handlebars are powerful, sinewy and strong, as muscular as if he'd escaped from one of those social-realist monuments our forefathers raised in the name of the proletariat, in the name of work, and our gazes meet just as I walk past the hairdresser who's smoking the day's first outside her salon and I wish her a good morning and she does the same and I walk a little further and come to the edge of the square where the alkies and addicts have already kicked off the day, and one of them laughs and smiles and says good morning and I say the same to her and her dude, who walks along a metre behind her pushing a bike with a punctured tyre, says good afternoon and laughs hoarsely and I shake my head at the lousy joke, but I'm happy, in some way, that they're happy, and I pass a stallholder unpacking their wares on the square and I keep walking, you know, I'm just walking along, down another street, looking at some teenagers smoking and drinking energy drinks, throwing the rattling aluminium cans on the pavement, two men come walking along from the wasteland where they sleep under tarpaulins strung between pallets, and one of them bends down and picks up a conker, weighs it in his hand, holds it, looks at it and throws it up again, up into the tree, up into the boughs of the tree, and it stays there, as though he was a fucking angel or something, maybe a demon, I don't know what the difference is – he throws it back into the tree, into its casing, onto its twig, its branch and trunk and down into this earthly hell and its burning core, and I close and open my eyes again, and see some dogs nosing and pissing, crying children who don't want to go to school, it's like I see, really *see* all this shit, this movement, you get me Cody? Can you grasp all that? I don't know, Cody, but this is where it all becomes so clear to me, so obvious that everything fits together, Cody, doesn't it, Cody? Maybe that's the thing, maybe that's what's so beautiful, as they say, perhaps it's that commonality, the fact we're heading in the same direction in some way, that we're waiting for the same bus, getting on the same bus and sitting there, standing on the escalator behind one another, heading down into the tunnels, sitting on the metro opposite one another, not speaking but exchanging looks, energies, touching the same objects and breathing the same air, out and in and out and in, all the time, round and round, I don't know, sure, it's hard and ugly and damaged and fucked up with drugs, but still nice to come home, that's what I mean, still nice to see your friends, your sisters, brothers, still beautiful to watch their struggle, every day, every night, it's beautiful, as they say, so yeah, you're right, it's beautiful, you're right even though you don't know what you're talking about, you've got no fucking clue, I didn't say of course, but should have, right Cody? And you say, yeah, yeah, Soot, calm down, and we crease up, and you say yeah, you're right about that, man, you should have said that, why didn't you say that? And I say I don't know, I suck my teeth, feel the gravel and the taste of blood, feel the pull of the THC, spit out the foam that's collected with my tongue in overdrive and point at my head and say Dezorient Express, man, and *Wait, ladies and gentlemen, please, my head's in a fog, I can't speak*, and so here we are again with that whole fucking cherry orchard shit, makes you wonder what kind of fucking orchard it is, what kind of cherries we're talking about here, where they're from, and I don't know, and I do that thing with my teeth again and say, you know, I've always been jealous of the people who don't end up rejecting their parents, I mean, the people who can respect their parents, and I don't mean cos they've inherited a summer house or something, but you know, because they were honest, honourable, hard-working, enlightened, you understand, strivers, and to be frank, well-brought-up middle-class, that's what we're talking about, you know, immigrants who, if they hadn't migrated, would have passed down summer houses in their wills, if you get me, thanks to my mum for teaching me to strive, and brush my teeth, and oh, thanks Dad, you taught me everything about combustion engines and philosophy, you taught me what it means to be proud and you taught my sister to stand up for herself, taught my brother to handle his drink and violence and shit, you get me Cody? Soot says, and I see him before me, Soot, I think about his sister, Vasti, we called her Cherry, after the fruit, or Neneh, I'm not sure, but it had nothing to do with Soot's orchards, nothing at all, but she was his sister and I think about how I went round to her place and the kitchen was all fucked up and I remember she wasn't crying any more, she just looked bitter and hard, cleaned up after him, the kids were with a neighbour. I said: who fucked up the cupboard doors, the plates, the glasses? And Cherry said: you know who. Soot, my brother, my own brother. My own flesh and blood. Almost everything in common. Our childhood. All these memories. Half our lives. More than that. And now. Now what? Psycho, homeless, drunk, pills, probably more, totally fucking p-noid. I'm not like him, at least. I take care of myself. And the kids. Nothing like him. None of us siblings like him. A little self-respect. Every day, we're striving. Taking care of ourselves, of each other. And who takes care of him? No one. That's the thing. Not him. And no one else can be fucked with it. We all feel bad, but no one can be fucked with it. Cherry cleared up, I helped her. I said: I know. I cut him off too. We blew up. Got into a fight. Almost. Didn't he tell you? He's frail, but he tried to attack me. It was night-time, outside the petrol station on Feldstrasse. By the entrance to the metro. We'd bought some beers and got into some beef. Can't remember why. I was holding his hands cos he was trying to attack me. I remember getting tunnel vision I was so angry. I could've killed him with my bare hands, I knew that. So I held onto his. I could only see him, his face, covered in mother-fucking adult acne. He went in, as though he was going to hit me, but I grabbed his wrists and held him there. I gripped hard. Really hard. It was hurting him. He started whining. I said if he tried to hit me one more time I'd do him in. Really. Then I let go. And you know. The thing was, my dad was standing a way off, watching. He didn't do anything. Just laughed nervously, acted worldly, drank a beer. But afterwards, Soot kept saying I'd hurt him without provocation. So bizarre. He showed everyone his wrists. And there were bruises. Of course. I'd been holding him hard. As I said. I'd been holding onto him hard instead of beating him to death. They were dark, almost black bruises. It was for his own sake, I did what was best for him, as they say. And he whined and whined. And my dad, who'd seen it all, said nothing, just said we should stop fighting, getting at each other. But after that I didn't speak to Soot for a while. So yeah, I distanced myself too. Cos of the fight, and cos he rang me up in the middle of the night. Wouldn't listen. And Cherry said: I know. Me too. Cos he stole from me. Cos he came here with his violence. Came here with his whores. I didn't want the kids to see that. They shouldn't have to see that shit. Not yet, anyway. At least, not more than they've already seen. Not as much as we've seen, you get me. I just got sick of it. Soot's psychotic babble. Soot's lies. Soot's attacks and accusations. Soot's cursing and filth. Mostly I didn't want him doing something to them. Not cos I think he would.

But you never know. I said: no, you never know. No, you never know with him. It's impossible to know. You just have to hope, cross your fingers, wait. Impossible to know. It depends. Cherry said: it all depends. It depends what he's high on, or not got hold of, who he's fallen out with. There's always a conflict. I said: always. And they can never be resolved, cos he needs them. I don't wanna sound like his psychologist or nothing. But, you know. And she said: no, I don't wanna sound like his bloody psychologist or nothing either, not that he's ever had one, to be fair, cos it's not that fucking easy, going to a psychologist, really, believe me, he'd never've managed more than two or three times, and taking it seriously, doing something about his problems? Forget it, but, you know, these conflicts can never be resolved and he needs them, because his perception of reality is totally different to other people's. I swear, his brain is totally fried, man. He's been stuffing those chemicals up into it since he was twelve, thirteen. Every day, pretty much. We're not living in the same world. And if that's the case, how can we even get along? There's no way of knowing. If he comes to see the kids, for instance. Has he got a knife today? Pepper spray? How can you live with him? How can you make it work? I can't. Not any longer. Not any more. You know, I said. You know: the sick thing is that I sometimes think there's no solution for these people and that we should actually exterminate them, for everyone's sake. So they can't cause any more suffering. Honestly. For themselves, for others. So they can't have any more children. So we don't have to see them fucking about with alcopops and pills pushing a pram in the morning when we're on the way to school or work. Cherry said: honestly? I said: I swear. But it's totally sick. I know, totally sick. But it's what I think, I swear. If they could just disappear. If I just didn't have to see. But that's not the point, that's just an impulse, some sort of mental mechanism or whatever you call it, a – I don't know – reaction, you get me, but as soon as I start thinking a little, you know, it passes, but what I mean is like, if *I* think that – I mean *me*, when my values are actually completely different, or whatever, my opinions are completely different, I think in a different way. You know, I'd never do anything like that, right, it's just a thought, a feeling, a reaction to something, to them, to their way of like totally taking over my life, right, a reaction to their threat – but I mean, what I mean is, if that's what *I* think, what do all those cop types think, all the ones who really have something to lose, all the ones who can actually act on their thoughts, you get me? Do you never think like that? Cherry said: I mean, you can't think like that. I said: I know, I can't help it. Cherry said: try. I heard the composer say: like almost seven hours of *The Well-Tuned Piano* or Riley's *In C*, though perhaps with pure intervals, you know, something like that, somewhere far away, and I noted, from the corner of my eye, that a yellow bus was driving towards us at full speed, and I skipped to one side slightly, a movement that was, I think, simultaneously intentional and reflexive. Or the impulse came from the line between reflex and intention, consciousness, if such a line exists. I don't know, the guitarist said, but it's so damned *American*, do you know what I mean, while someone like Julius Eastman never had a chance. Exactly, the composer said, and why do you think that was the case? Why were some worshipped and praised while others fell into abuse and homelessness before dying in obscurity? But you know, Soot, I hear myself say, instead of replying to the composer, because I always have to defend him, always have to say something nice about Soot, always try and find some positive angle, always stand up for him even though he maybe doesn't deserve it, even though he's a filthy *blatte* tramp, as I once heard Vasti say on the phone to a friend, but you know, I begin to say, think about it, he hasn't always been like this, when we were little he was smart, interested in things, like any kid. You want to grow, to learn in some way, develop, but he was too young to start using, it destroyed him, I say, your parents were fucked up, I say, with their own shit, how was he going to manage, but yeah, I know, it's not that simple, at some point he has to take responsibility for his own actions, at some point it's on him, I know, and now I'm gesticulating, in my head at least, starting to move differently, in, like, some inner body, I know, I know, I also came close to beating him to a pulp, the little bastard, but he can't just do whatever he feels like, behave however he wants, with no respect, but you know, I think, it could all have been different, right, why shouldn't it have been different? But how, how, I don't know, you know, but it didn't start off like this, it was different before it got like this, he was different before he got like this, and I go on talking, more and more and round and round, words and words and words till I end up with that cherry orchard stuff, and you know, I can just hear Soot's voice saying cherry orchard blah blah blah, are you thick in the head, bro, fuck that, he's laughing, his laughter sounds like Tupac's hoarse voice, give it up, just give it the fuck up, you fool, I'm done listening to your shit, your voice is hurting my brain, you get me. It's done, it's already over. Too late. You can't think like that, Cherry said. Well in that case everything's better the way it is. It doesn't get any better, it doesn't get any easier or clearer. But I do, you know. I just do. I walk past that square every day. Every morning, every afternoon. Every weekday, and often on the weekends too. I see them every time. I don't know their names, but I recognise the faces, the old Yugo with the ponytail, you know, the Polish woman with no teeth, the skinny bug-eyed Turk, the hard rocker who's always laughing, then those two small-time dealers, the twins, what are they: Latinos, Arabs, I dunno, but always dressed in those Adidas trackies. Almost every day I see them. As soon as the hostel throws them out each morning, they're there. And I think about him, maybe even miss him. And? What do you mean? I mean, OK, the crux, the central point, what is it? That it could have been us? That it could have been me? Sure, that's the truth. It doesn't get any more banal than that. It's true. It's a place that I was destined for and that I escaped. This hangdog thing. The drugs, the crime, the death. Doing time, filthy mattresses and sofas, the hostels, the psych wards, the memorial gardens. The whole shebang. That life and that death. It's true. But what does it mean? What do you think it means? Sure. Yeah. You're right. It's not some kind of straightforward survivor guilt, if that's what you were thinking. What I feel is only partly sympathy, empathy, understanding. I also want to smash their faces in. They disgust me. Have you ever seen someone have a breakdown? Close up? The weakness, the bodily fluids, the shamelessness, the spiritual and intellectual poverty. How pathetic it is. How ridiculous it is. Self-hatred, you say? Wannabe psychologist. OK, maybe a bit. There's a limit. It's the limit that you see. It's the line between human and animal. But actually I think it's extremely weird that it hasn't occurred to anyone to just get rid of them. They don't fulfil any function, the poor, the ones not needed in the factories, the ones not needed on the production line, in the care system, for cannon fodder, for brothel fodder, why has no one systematised this, an organised extermination of unnecessary lives, used up or unusable, a drain, why isn't there an extermination camp for them, I don't get it, even I've thought that thought, even me, who could've been one of them, like I'm saying, it's a place, I'll say it over and over, till the meaning is clear, till the meaning, the true significance of these words, crystallises, till something unpronounceable becomes manifest, in some as yet indescribable way, yeah, I'll say it again, it's a place that I was destined for and that I escaped and if even I think it might be best to just get rid of them, the way people do with stuff they've no more use for, the way people do with animals that no longer fill a function, it's true, what many people say: anything you can do to an animal, to a rat, a dog, a monkey, anything you can do to an animal you can do to a human, that thing about human life having a value in itself is ridiculous, in this context it's ridiculous, bizarre, absurd, almost nauseating it's such bullshit, anything you can do to a rat you can do to a human, and you can do anything to a rat, and when I walk past the square, every morning, every afternoon, and on the weekends now and then, with friends or alone, and see them, their faces, and recognise them, without knowing their names, though I recognise their faces, their bodies – every single time I

think all this, these lives, why hasn't it occurred to anyone
to just get rid of them, or rather, why has no one put it
into action yet, these thoughts exist, in my head, and no
doubt in their heads, suicide is a solution too of course,
a funeral is much cheaper than all that care, all that
rehab, all those police initiatives, building all those prisons, maintaining them and on and on and on. All that
palliative care, to no end. Anything you can do to an
animal you can do to a human. Yeah, I'm sure it will
happen, said Cherry, I'm sure we'll see it one day, she
said, looking pained. The pictures show a street that
would seem completely unremarkable to you, but which
is a veritable oasis in their desert, said the photographer,
Riis, to the group of benefactors. It's surrounded in every
direction by densely packed dirt and many streets, hum-
ming with a young, wretched, squalid generation. But its
pavement is comparatively free of those children who
have nowhere but the street to play, which creates a
rather desolate impression, because so few people walk
there. Yeah. Anything you can do to a rat you can do to
a human, and you can do whatever you want to a rat.
Yeah, Cody, said Soot, that's how it has to be, and soon
we'll die, like rats, sinking down, leaving, becoming
something else, lost. Yes, leaving. The world, life – these
concepts aren't important any more. Earth, the part that's
not water, the continents, the nation, the landscape, the
city, the district, the building, the room, the bed. The
washing-up unwashed, the pan rusting, the bread going
stale, the butter melting. Sickbed, sickness. It's night, I'll
do a few lines and, an hour later, a few more, those will
be the last. Place is everything and death is placelessness
to us. Bodilessness. We're the confined ones, we're the

ones incapable of using our gifts. Despair, sorrow, loneliness. Insomnia creates new spaces, pockets of time, has
a unique light, unique sounds, how they appear depends
on where you live, the way everything depends on where
you live. Soot is awake when everyone else is sleeping.
And vice versa. Soot is a reflection of something, a reflection, an inside-out being, an interior on the surface, the
outside within him, a whole world in there, a world of
reactions, effects, consequences. Soot says suicide is not
an alternative. Soot repeats it, suicide is no alternative.
Soot has his place, in front of the window, in front of and
above the street lights, and it doesn't resemble anything:
no photos, no films, no books and no games, none of the
sci-fi white corridors, no dark-as-night shit, no romantic
rock songs and no hip-hop diss tracks with pumping
basslines from the clubs of the American South, it really
doesn't resemble anything. I don't even resemble myself.
I look at myself, as though from the outside, from the
future: afterwards I thought I should have known something would go wrong that day. That I should have felt it
coming. Wasn't that the case? Wasn't everything that
morning steeped in a foolish good humour? Wasn't there
something beautiful and docile, almost benevolent about
the late-morning skies, about the building facades gliding
past outside the bus, about all the central-station bustle,
the people in the cafes, the stacks of newspapers and
chocolate, the weight of the railway lines, the landscape,
which, as unassuming as it was tyrannical, opened up
outside the train window. Soft drinks, coffee, cinnamon
buns. Birches, houses, fields. A jokey text (someone was
looking forward to 'corybantic ecstasies'). A bird that
seemed to sing for me alone. That sensuality, in living. A

soft scarring. The body faced with this love, yeah an address, a message of love, why ever not, that had previously been concealed, now came forth into the light. And this light flooded, heavy and urgent, over objects and beings, over the world, whose age and size were so enormous that the mere hint of it, the mere hint of the contours of just an insignificant fraction of all that, of the unnameable fabric of eternity, that boundless cloud of not knowing, had me drowning in love. Somewhere there, in formulations like this, in the affect of love, in its simplicity. At this point I should have thought: something's going to happen. It's going to hurt. I'm going to hurt. In the darkness of our era: in a constantly expanding universe, where the distance that separates us from the most distant galaxies grows at a speed that means their light can never reach us, it's our job to become aware, in the darkness, of that light that is trying to reach us and can't. That's our task, when heavy raindrops fall on the earth at dawn, and we hear the muted sound of them boring down into the soft, loose stuff of the furrows, a roguish bird flies just above the ground, mimicking a child's cry, and the rain relents as the light intensifies, and the air is fresh and clear, and in the earth puddles glimmer before sinking down, and animals peer out, among them the human animal. The human animal looks proud. Here, she says to her crying children. Eat and live, and she presses them against her body. They don't know how but they soon learn. They learn fast. They find paths. They learn. They spread. They look at each other. They say: we're living. They die, and bury one another. Cities grow. They say: we live here. In the city centres, near the squares and the parks, near the meadows, the fields. We've lived long with the fields. You can see it in our bodies, our skins. We sit and watch the night and tell of everything we've seen. We saw the rains come. We lived with the animals. We watched them be fed and die. We ate them and we buried them. We gave them names. We lived with the machines. We oiled and repaired them. We had names. We screamed our names. Day and night. Called out our names. Let the night envelop me, we begged. And we invoked fires. Now we sit on balconies, looking out over the burning hills and fields. We sit and smoke and drink liquor and listen to the radio and look out at those roguish birds mimicking the children's cries and we're still starting fires. We drink liquor and say: the skull, that is what a girl is called in the nomads' language. The outline of her skeleton showed in her worn features. The skull tells us: once I would take my children with me from city to city, in cages, in containers. On the backs of their necks I wrote their names and birthplaces. The cemetery from the First World War: that's where I saw the names mixed up, saw that everything was mingled. The skull was my great-grandmother, she came from the Eastern Side, and she used to say that on the night I was born she'd seen a dark star in the sky. My family talked about it a lot when I was young, about what it might mean; what Great-grandmother had actually meant by *star*. It wasn't until many years later, when I was on the way to becoming a grown man and Great-grandmother was dead, when the whole Eastern Side had disappeared, or at least the Eastern Side that had been hers, when the outer wall had been moved and the Eastern Side was under the sway of the new Ruler, it wasn't until then that we even began to ask ourselves what she meant by *dark*, because it was now clear that the Eastern Side's darkness, Great-grandmother's darkness, wasn't the same as ours. Your name, Cody, she said, the skull said, shortly before she died, your name made me recall how I used to carry around a cranium I'd found in an old chapel. I carried it from city to city. They'd moved graves and exposed 100-year-old skeletons. On the skulls they wrote the names and birthplaces of the deceased. I used to focus my gaze downwards, at the ground, at the obstacles in my way, the puddles and at the bumps in the asphalt, where I thought I saw something of significance. The bumps in the asphalt and the cheekbones were painted with roses and forget-me-nots. Carnations and wax plants. That's what my great-grandmother said, now she's like a skull inside my head, a cranium full of names, dates, flowers. In that way, perhaps some aspect of the Eastern Side's world view lives on. Now I'm weightless, looking up. Through the roof, which is open to the sky, I see swarms of thrushes flying by, birds that rise in the dusk before darkness closes the routes available to them. I remember the suicide scenes in the tower-block landscape of my childhood, that magical hall of mirrors. It drove me mad. What was it that drove me mad? The wealth of variations? Or the opposite, this alone, this monolithic fact? The thing that drove me mad, the thing that pulled me out of my childishly straightforward, simple existence, out of my wits, was the realisation – at first diffuse, covert and inexplicable, before becoming a revelation and then a kind of experience, a somatically and intellectually couched understanding – that some lives don't deserve to be lived. That this lie prevails. And no one can do anything about it. Images flicker. Something glimmers. When I was a kid,

there was a four-year-old boy who lived on the ground
floor of the house across the street from us. I'll call him
Antonio. Of course he was called something else, but
these kinds of anecdote always have, by necessity, a degree
of impossibility, so I'm unable to tell you his real name.
Once I saw Antonio eating polystyrene. He would sometimes stand there, pissing out of his bedroom window,
wearing his too-big cowboy boots. And he used to say he
fucked his little sister. If there was a fight in the yard,
and there often was when Antonio was around, he would
try to frighten his enemies by saying they should watch
out – because his dad worked at the prison. One of my
classmates lived two floors above Antonio. We can call
him Olof, though he too was called something else,
equally unmentionable. Because he was short and very
scrawny, people round there used to prefix his name with
the word Little. So we can say he was called Little Olle. I
never caught sight of Little Olle's dad, perhaps he worked
with Antonio's dad, I don't know, but his mum was also
short and very skinny. She was out of work and an addict.
What she took I don't know, I never got that close. Once
when I went to Little Olle's house to play the computer
game *Pong* the whole flat had been emptied of furniture.
We went into the kitchen. It smelled vile, and in the
middle of the floor, where the kitchen table had previously been, was now a large black bin liner. It was well
filled, that much I can remember, but however much I
try, I can't recall what it contained. Nor can I remember
if we found out what had happened to the furniture. But
I think it was probably the bailiffs who'd been there
to collect things that, in the eyes of the state, could
have been put to better use, or maybe his mum had sold

everything worth selling to get the money for something that was more important at that moment. I don't know, it's like my memory just stops. Something comes to a halt there in the kitchen and the room closes around us; two children of about ten in front of a black bin bag with indeterminate contents that reaches their chins. An image. That flashes up for a moment. And then what? Unveils its significance? Never to be seen again? Can the past really be captured that way? How can you reconcile that volatility with the enormity and persistence of that experience? And what is true in this shifting moment? Whose truth, whose history? I don't know. I only know that I'm tied to it. And there's always more to be said about it. There's always more of it. Even when it's quiet. It's so quiet. The days pass. No, the days fall. Slowly, like softly fluted petals. Weeks, months, years. We grow older. We forget one another, the contours of our faces fade and we remember other things entirely. Everything shape-shifts, over and over. In the end we don't know what's true, what's false, where one thing starts and the next finishes, or what one thing has to do with the next. What ideas about power and freedom – ideas about the tension between possibility and necessity – have to do with that bin bag, that room. With the shifting image of Antonio's cowboy boots and the crumbs of polystyrene in the corner of his mouth. It's more than just images, I force myself to write. It's more than just words. There's always more. Behind every voice a choir. A flicker of bodies. If I listen I hear. The sound carves into the walls. Through the window, secured with a substantial padlock, I see the men gathering, a dozen young men helping each other remove the barbed wire before the police return. I remember it being beautiful in the dawn and the dusk. Almost every day I fantasise about gruesome violence, that I'm going to kill a pig with my bare hands. A man. My enemy, sometimes I think he looks like me. Through the tunnels, whose lighting no longer works, we are transported, in a stolen factory-fresh Renault, and I think of steel-blue mountains beyond rose gardens, of small islands appearing in the dawn light, fields lying fallow. I suddenly remember, out of nowhere, an enormous and mystifying lightness. One thing I've learned: to beware of calling time and society by their true names. To make your way as though through a bad dream: without looking left or right, with lips pressed tight together and gaze fixed. When you're locked in it's easier to cry. I'm silent, my lips pressed tight together and my gaze fixed. Oh, swathe me in night and surround me with holy pyres. Was that a prayer? Was it Soot who was praying? Let me fall for all time a victim, but by Your hand only. Yes, he was praying. In the evenings, lying in bed, the ceiling and the cold light from the window, sidelong. Hand folded on his chest. Yes, even that. *Our Father who art in heaven*. Like a child. It's almost a joke. *Miserere Mei, Deus*. In a cell. That's how Soot died. Yes, exactly, and that's particularly clear in *Antiphona nach Hildegard von Bingen*, the guitarist said at this point, in a kind of triumphal tone I just couldn't get my head around, probably because I'd missed something central to his argument, but it was something to do with the difference between bordun and ostinato, and at that same moment we heard a loud bang behind us, and a strange, unplaceable sound, kind of metallic and sharp, but also wet, fleshy, and then, without really understanding, I realised what it was and I turned round

91

and knew then that I'd also heard a braking sound: screeching brakes or tyres skidding across asphalt or something similar, and some kind of hissing, venting sound, and what I saw was a bus positioned diagonally across the carriageway, and in front of that bus lay a person and a bicycle, all wrapped around each other, behind one of the front wheels, it was difficult to tell exactly what I was looking at, like my brain couldn't make sense of the image, and I heard a whimpering sound, and saw a woman in an orange coat running over to the body, to offer help, I assume, I saw her almost bounding over to the front part of the bus and bending over, but then she kind of flinched back, as though an invisible force had repulsed her, or pulled her back, she turned her gaze and her face away from what she saw under the bus, and her hands moved, shook, in a peculiar, irregular way in front of her face and I saw that we'd come closer, without noticing I'd set my bike aside, leaning it against the bridge railing, and moved towards the site of the accident, which had now attracted a dozen or so other people, and in among them the bus driver paced back and forth and I saw his face, that drained, grey, tired face, the white short-sleeved shirt and the red tie, and I saw several people had gone over to the victim and got out their phones, so I stopped, realising the guitarist and the composer were stood alongside me, it must have been four or five metres from the front wheel of the bus, I couldn't stop myself looking, and now I saw the black jacket, the black hood, blood and something white sticking out, between shredded clothes and bicycle parts, and I averted my gaze. It was him, I thought, it's him, the junkie, it's him, he's lifeless.

Wax plants? Was it really wax-plant flowers I was thinking of as I stood there by the canal, against the backdrop of the police station's symmetrical facade? Wasn't it cherry blossoms? And it wasn't at home on the windowsill that I'd seen them, was it, but in the yard, in the garden, by the fence, wasn't that it? Or in the park, past the bridge, under the bridge, yeah, in the water, in the cold, dark water, bobbing, calm and serene. We should go, said the guitarist after a while. I don't know how much time had passed, but it was enough for the full realisation to hit us that there was nothing we could do, nothing at all. We saw the paramedics come and deal with the body, someone else was looking after the driver, and several times I was about to open my mouth and say something, that I'd met that guy before, just a little while ago, just before you came, by the canal, by the police station, but for some reason I couldn't manage it, didn't know where to begin, from which end, from which sensory impression, and now the guitarist was silent too, and the composer just said *Jesus*, and *fucking hell*, a few times, and we walked to the central station, bought our tickets and took the escalator down to the platforms. We drifted down and I felt like I was having to shout to make myself understood, even though the guitarist and the composer were standing right next to me, so close I could hear them breathe, hear the swishing and rustling of their clothes. This is how it is, I thought several times, more or less involuntarily, and without even knowing what that meant. *This is how it is. This is my life. It has to be this straightforward. So tyrannical. The junkie's dead and I'm the only one left.* Then I thought, still on the escalator, going down and down and down, that it was idiotic, that my thoughts were idiotic, that I was an idiot. And we got on the train, in silence. The guitarist got out his phone and started tapping at it. I looked at the composer, she closed her eyes and sort of massaged them, rubbed her fingers against her eyelids, and I took the chance to lean my head back and close my eyes too, my hands resting on my lap as the train glided across the Øresund. We got off at Nørreport and wandered across to the cathedral. The guitarist said something about a car accident he'd been involved in where everyone had escaped with their lives, and the composer showed us a scar she'd got when a car she'd been in drove into a motorway barrier. We reached the church, paid the entrance fee and sat right at the front on the left-hand side, each with a programme in our hands. Then Christoph Maria Moosmann entered. I turned round, looked up at the organ and could just make him out as he sat down at the manual. He began to play Pärt's *Annum per Annum* and everything seemed to close in, filling with weight and levity, the room expanded and contracted as though it were breathing, and I breathed with it, and a few seconds into the first chord's powerful vibrations I breathed out, before holding, lungs empty, for the rest of the minute the chord sounded. Then it ebbed away, and I drew breath, deeply and noisily, much too noisily in the quiet church, as though I'd been underwater and was now struggling up to the surface, up to the oxygen, just as the pause, the silence, was at its most intense, and when those first weak, light, playfully searching notes began to sound I couldn't help once again thinking about Soot and about that last night, about what I'd done, what I was, about Kiko and Rawna, about that bus, on that roundabout, that circular motion and the centrifugal force that pushed me out towards everything with such satanic power. We were supposed to be going out and having it, as we used to say, and we'd chilled at Kiko's, and then onwards, met Dima, Becky, Argo, Saima, Fernanda, I don't know who else, Hansson maybe, Zoltan, Vadim, and were heading up to Elsa V's to get some shit, do a quick job for her. We dropped one there straight off, but had to wait an hour at least before she let us in, seemed there was a lot of people passing through, a lot going on. She gave us the gear and we took off in search of Slovak, the Bulgarian. A few evenings before, I'd been sitting in Arben's crappy Mazda 323, with its driving ban, waiting for Hansson, who was running around trying to sell those nine-bars from Christiania, and the radio was playing some new song by some new rapper and Arben said to Kiko, who was sitting there grooving and nodding along, that he hated those fuckin gangsta fuckers, as he put it, that whole thug style, he said, what even is that, *ey hey yo waddup, man's glidin in the whip,* he mocked, *the screen's all tinted, guy's fuckin minted, let's go, shorty's so damn wet,* with a retarded expression, *suit's got three stripes, but my cock's so crooked, nigga speak real funny, all this coke got me cookin,* and we laughed and I said cuz dem bars is on fire, but he was being serious, said damn I fucking hate them, I swear, I mean actually living that life is one thing, not saying nothing bout that, but bragging bout it, chatting shit that way, tricking the kids into thinking everything's cool blingbling, it's bullshit, man, it's totally wack, no joke, and Kiko thought he should calm down, it's just music, he said, but Arben said it's more than that, it's advertising a lifestyle, and anyone who's seen that life at all knows it's 90 per cent stress, he said, and I said he'd just said it was better to live that life than to rap about it, but that's not what I mean, he said, you know yourself it's 90 per cent chaos, but Kiko said hey, what you chatting about, per cent this per cent that as if you work in a bank or something, course it can be stressful but there are quiet times too, admit it, who gives a shit if it's not bling, but Abbe insisted, listen man, 90 per cent panic, he said, believe me, all night long when you're on your own and can't sleep and your mates, your fucking brothers, could stab you in the back at any moment, for nothing, and not even for the cash, not for some tinted whip, man, for nothing, just cos they're scared and tired too and they have to play the fucking game, honest to god, Tony Montana this and that, such fucking thug chat, I can't even hear it, has anyone ever even seen the whole of that film, don't they know how it ends, and I said *you think you kill me with bullets? I take your fucking bullets!* and Kiko was bent double with laughter and told Arben he should become a politician, or work for Save the Children or something, don't you realise it's art, bro, music, and what you're saying's not true, loads of people tell you how bad that life is, rap about stress and suicide, even Biggie and that lot did, but you know what, they have to be hard and real at the same time, you know, they have to have respect from the streets, and Arben opened the window and spat. Real, go fuck your mother, he said, this is real, and then he pulled up his shirt and showed us the scars under his arm, but I don't go around acting like some fucking monkey, and Kiko grinned and said yeah yeah, bro, you're hard, but you're no gangster, you're a fucking small-time thief, man, a bike thief, and you're getting old, fifteen-year-old kids rob you, so don't take this the wrong way, bro, but who's gonna rap about that, about being stressed out and poor, unemployed poly-addict, failure among failures, you get me, homie, I mean, just look at your car, man, not exactly an advert for your lifestyle, and Abbe looked pissed and said we could get out if it was so shit, and just when I thought they were gonna start fighting for real, Hansson turned up and said the guy didn't want to pay and also we were probably being watched now cos that fucking idiot didn't warn us. And surprise, surprise, we got stopped by the pigs three minutes later. They lined us up by the nursery school, right in front of the kids and staff, all staring, frisked us and searched the Mazda. They impounded the car but none of us were carrying anything, so they had to let us go. Then we rang Dima, who came after half an hour and drove us home, he dropped me off last and that's when I found out why Arben had been so pissed. His dad had got his sentence and was going down for eighteen months. I thought I'm gonna cheer him up, so I rang and said, mate, I've got a bottle of Bacardi, want to pick up some Coke and come over and have a few, *estilo cubano*? He laughed at me and said, stop being a dick. I said what? He said he couldn't be bothered, he was going to drop a

few benzos and watch a film or something. *Estilo cubano*,
he said. You're totally thick in the head, man. Two hours
later Hansson rang. He'd sold the nine-bars. Time to get
paid, bro. Are you in for the next round? And I didn't
really want to any more, but I thought about the first
time we'd gone over to Christiania to buy up the stuff
and everyone was there apart from Marko who chickened
out, we'll get banged up, he said, and if we don't get
banged up we'll get taxed by one of the big guns. We said
your lookout, man, more green for us then, and then
everything went fine, no problem at all, and we made a
bit, not that much but still, you know, a bit extra, while
he had all these different jobs, official, unofficial, legal;
but he was still poor and trying to get his grades and all
that, and in the end he went to some club to chill out,
but this psycho-bouncer started hassling him till Marko
flipped out and then he got five or six months for aggra-
vated assault. I went in to see him the first week he was
there and he said he regretted fighting back, said it was
pointless, you always get it wrong, regardless. Then I'm
suddenly standing there in front of Elsa again with the
team behind me. What's up? She looks me in the eye,
then at the faces surrounding me. You've brought your
friends, she says. New faces. As long as they're halal. Dima
giggles with nerves. I give Elsa the money. She's got her
tiger face on. She casts a glance at the notes, folds them
once and stuffs them in her pocket. I reach out my hand.
The others giggle too. Thanks, I say, a little too quickly,
before she's given me anything. Same to you, she says,
taking my hand in hers. Enjoy responsibly. I put the bags
away and the wraps the kids had folded for her. Then she
gets out the big packet and a dark-blue rucksack, she

passes both over. Give this to Slovak and he'll give you the money. Be careful. You can go out that way in a minute, the others have just gone, she says, and points to the door in the back. Thanks, I say. Yep, you already said that. Relax, it's cool. She grins and turns round. She has a big scar on her upper arm. It says *DOOM* on her top. We go out, and then into the club again via a door guarded by this absolutely enormous guy with an Ivan Drago hairdo, black polo shirt and a fat gold chain over his shirt. Want something to drink? Becca says to me. Nah, it's cool, I say. Then she tells me about this guy who'd tried to play the hero. He'd come by a little money, she says, said he wanted to take me out to dinner. We went to some place, kind of like a falafel joint but a bit nicer, with Persian food. We ate this beautiful rice he liked, then he said he was going to take care of me. He promised, you know, all formal. I'm gonna protect you, he said. He said with him around I'd never come to harm. And to be honest I felt grossed out. I looked at him. Then I took a fork and stabbed myself in the arm. It made four holes and they were pretty deep. We just sat there a while. It was bleeding and he looked hurt. Almost desperate. It felt lonely. For both of us, I'm guessing. He tried to eat the rest of his food, but I just drank a bit and held a napkin against my arm. Then I said I should go home and disinfect the wound. Can I come along, he asked. And I felt like sticking the fork in his eye. But instead I just said of course. We laugh at the guy. I get up. I'm going for a piss, wait for me. I hate this UV light. Weird that she thought we were cops. She can't seriously have thought that, for fuck's sake. How you doing, Cody? I'm fine, I'm fine. You've got blood on your knuckle. On your knuckles. It's dripping.

Shit. I didn't notice. Sorry. What happened? Nothing. Did you get any on you? Here, tissue. How's it going? It's fine, it's cool. Stop asking the whole time, I'm getting spooked with you asking me that the whole damn time. How are you doing yourself? Cool. A bit glazed-over, dunno. Sorry. How are we gonna find the Slovak anyway? He's not a Slovak. He's just called Slovak, he's like Hungarian, or Bulgarian or something, I dunno, a filthy pimp in any case. Is everyone here? We're here. Did you get the bags? Yeah. And the nine-bars? Yeah, I got everything. What are they up to in there? Come on, let's go. We have to test it. We go to the pub, some wack place with darts and a slot machine and football on the TV and we order beer and cider and Dima goes into the toilet to test it. Comes out and you can see straight away it's a good high. Makes a ker-ching sign with his arm and then my turn and everything is suddenly dazzling, you know, the way it gets. One morning Soot woke up on the floor of his apartment in Pruitt-Igoe. He'd managed to smash all the window-panes in the apartment and now the cold wind was blowing in over the shards. His hands were bloody, his knuckles all torn, on one of them something white, cartilage or bone, was showing. It made him dizzy to look at it. In the kitchen he washed his face and, carefully, the backs of his hands. Then he went out into the bathroom and started gathering things up from the floor. When he'd gathered up all his toiletries and towels and jewellery, he took the shards of mirror and put them in a large glass jar he'd brought in from the kitchen. First the big shards, then the smaller ones, then the very smallest with a broom and last of all he hoovered up the tiny, barely visible slivers and grains, with the old vacuum cleaner he'd stolen from a building site a year or two back. Then he grabbed a damp cloth and wiped away most of the blood from the walls and the floor. Same thing in the living room and the bedroom. His wounds stung and burned. Cherry came by. She looked around and gave him a hard stare. Maybe you should get that bandaged up, she said, nodding at his hands. A sound came from his throat. He picked up a butt from the floor and lit it. It'll be cold now, Cherry said. You look different. Different? Not different. Not really. No. There's nothing different. Things are things. Yeah. The future's already here, it's just unevenly distributed. Trippy, bro. You get me? No. I dunno. Or maybe. I think. Wait, come on. Let's go. Let's get out of here. In the car. Away. Up. Down. No fucking clue where. Out. And why shouldn't there be slum lenses, Riis says up on the stage, when there are lenses for other purposes, like portrait, landscape and architecture. 'Slum' can, from our particular perspective, be defined as a narrow, dark yard with a number of wretched women and children hanging about the doorways – especially in good weather. Because of the high surrounding buildings and the narrow passageways, the light that falls on this kind of group is so weak and poor that brighter optics than normal are required to produce an exposure. Until lenses suitable for slum conditions are available, all we can recommend is the use of strong achromatic lenses. This is an area for further research, which will reward anyone who gets to grips with the problem – now the season is approaching. Some heavies threatened to rape Becca and I didn't dare say anything. Woke up in the afternoon, somewhere else. The day vanished quickly, I helped Katti procure a little paper, as she called it, lit some incense, sandalwood, outside the door, fucking hippy, said Dima, people passed on the long balcony, as Sanne calls the walkways, the children were playing football and skipping, we ate scrambled eggs with our hands from a big frying pan, licked each other's fingers, before slumping onto the sofa to play PlayStation. Fell asleep like that, dreamed I could suck myself off. The next day I met Kiko down by the shops, he had some isolator, and we smoked a tiny little bit, stupidly. I got so zonked I shit myself. Literally. I sat under a cafe table and shat my pants. I had to throw them away. Borrowed someone's boxers. We got kicked out of the place by some goody-goody lefties. Then we wandered around freezing our arses off. We met Hansson and Adi, who offered us some vodka, and thanks to them we ended up at some party where this pumped-up dude on acid was going round in a tight shirt with a face full of acne, talking shit. Everyone was fucked, but him most of all. Wired chats about anthill architecture and intelligent insects and illuminati bankers – Adi got hung up on the latter and it got too much for me. That guy was freaking me the fuck out and I told Sanne and she said me too, so we decided to do one, even though there were chicks and Suedi wanted to bang one of them. But first I stole a pair of trackies. Katti nicked a bunch of CDs, a bottle of gin and a whole box of fucking Cornettos. I realised I'd had enough and wanted to go home now, but instead we wandered around for a while, getting cold. The ice creams didn't help. We gave the rest to a beggar who stank of piss and he made a weird face. Then we got on the bus. Everyone started talking about football. Kiko gave a few guys the evil eye but nothing happened. I got noid. Adi started going on about some film with some kind of lizard goats or goat lizards and agents with telepathic beams and X-ray vision, a Medusa with her crew of snakes. I felt like eyes were staring at me. Sat on the bus unable to move. I was cold and my mouth was full of sugar that was somehow swelling up. I felt sick, and Becca said how the fuck do I manage to put up with this, for real? And I giggled a bit but Adi laughed until he cried and sang like a little kid about eejits who don't give a shit. Then he started babbling about his illuminati crap again, about this and that person owning this and that, and I said to him are you a nazi or something, man, look at your pants, and the whole time the bus was turning round and round, like a fucking carousel, and stopping and accelerating and stopping and accelerating, and suddenly I felt better, and I creased up about Adi's trashed whizz-head jeans, and Becca went for it and said look at your jacket, the three stripes, man, what kind of uniform is that anyway, I don't get it, mate, makes no difference where you are, which country, rich or poor, everyone has those three stripes on their pants, on their shirts, on their jackets, sweaters, on their shoes, unless they've got a swoosh, or whatever it's called, but didn't you know they were nazis, those Adidas boys, I swear, the name of the guy who started the whole thing was Adolf, he was called Adi, just like you, mate, it's like Adolf and Adnan are the same somehow, you get me, for some reason it's become a fucking gangster uniform all over the world, people who live in some ice-cold shithole in Outer Siberia wander around wearing sweaty vests and bumbags full of the kind of shit we throw in the bin – and you know they go around in like, sliders, even though it's below freezing outside, like that guy, you know, Ibbe, with his fucking prison slippers all year round, even they have their Adidas copies, made of, like, melted recycled plastic in some poisonous Chinese factory where everyone has cancer from the toxins in the air and the food and the water and the fags made out of like the roots of the tobacco plant or some shit, and in the end the poisons are in the gear too of course, gear they send out to their legion of piss-poor mates, of *lófasz*-gangsters, tramps who think that having three stripes on their clothes makes them kings, please, man, you're just giving free advertising to a company started by a nazi, I'm telling you, bro, it's nothing more than that, just cos some guy in the eighties went around rapping in Adidas garms, now all of you gotta have em, but fuck, you could just put a big clock round your neck like that dude from Public Enemy, why don't you do that, she said, and Adi made a weird noise with his tongue and just said fuck off, get lost, and I said haven't you got a better argument, you've got to disarm this shit she's talking, are you a soldier or a tramp? But he just said shut up you fuckin *mudak*, and there was a long silence and I felt so tired I could've fallen asleep anywhere, completely zonked, and then Adi turned to us, grinning from fucking ear to ear, saying stop being cunts and listen a sec, and he told us about his ABC book, he called it *The ABC of Storytelling*, which everyone thought was fucking dull, about A, who's 'telling a story in which B orates on the way C talks about D describing how E chattered on about F's retelling of that time G'd rambled on about the way H related how I'd extolled J's criticism of K's way of announcing that L had posited that M had whispered something about N's tendency to declare that O sometimes lisps on about the fact that P's spoken about Q

mumbling something about R's assertion that S once said
that T confirmed the fact that U pointed out that V noted
W's habit of gossiping about the time X yelled that Y
implied Z should stop lying about what kind of stories A
is telling', and the idea was that Soot would illustrate it,
but he didn't know how you would illustrate something
like that, because *nothing happens, you know*, it's just talk,
there's no images, so he just drew and sketched some
grotesque faces with great open mouths within mouths,
gobs within gobs, he said, with tongues, teeth, palates,
throat holes or whatever they're called, black holes telling
and questioning and complaining and declaring and
whispering and asserting and on and on, over and over
again, round and round, like a goddamn loop, said Soot,
like one of those staircases, you know, that just go up and
up in an eternal circle, and when Soot showed Hansson
those drawings, those sketches, he said cool, you've got
talent, but you know, you should do something simpler
so the man on the street can appreciate it, you get me,
something straighter, clearer, and Soot took the pad back,
pretended to gob on the floor and said stop chatting shit,
bro, I am the fucking man on the street, you goddamn
donkey, and Hansson opened his eyes wide and said OK,
man, chill, so draw something the donkey on the street
will understand then, and Soot shook his head and now
everyone was shooting sideways glances at Adi, and someone shouted *ayde, yalla*, we need to get off and then we
jumped off and within a few seconds we were in a fight
with some beggar tramp by the ATM and someone lost
it a bit and I shouted *who the hell are you to me, I'll bang your
whole family you bastard* to some filthy Italian squatters
who hadn't showered in months, they sleep with their

dogs, I said to Becca, I swear, fucking lousy shits, genuine vermin, filth, and then I admitted that OK, I haven't showered for a few weeks either, and laughed, got a crusty white cheesy bellend, I know, and she said why are you telling me that, you animal, do you want me to shove a tampon in your mouth? Allow it, don't talk like a whore, Adi said. Oi, *rassclaat*, watch it, said Saima, don't talk like a cop. Everyone laughed, I was nearly done for by this point, exhausted, but the pavement was like a conveyor belt, it was impossible to stop. We passed Lehmitz, went in, had a few tequilas, a bender in leather pants was standing on the bar playing air guitar to Judas Priest and Adi was jumping up and down like a proper mong, shriek-ing *thug life, thug life*, and Becca told this joke where you had to ask a cop if he or she, that is, they, you know, spoke French, and if you were lucky and they said yes, you asked them what nine was in French and then they'd say *neuf*, and then you'd say what? and they'd say *neuf* again, and if you'd filmed it you could just edit it together so you had a nice little sequence of them doing an impres-sion of a pig, and she laughed but then made a serious face and said shall we burn down the cop shop, but no one heard her cos the others were talking the whole time, I closed my eyes and pressed my eyelids and it was like I had a lava lamp in there, then I looked around for Kiko but couldn't see him. Kiko! Where are you? Kiko! There was red and green and white slime floating slowly around, I felt a bit sick but was trying to ignore it, everyone was shouting and again Becca said fuck we should burn the bacon factory, but no one heard and then a third time fuck the five-o and shouldn't we go and burn the fuckin pigsty to the ground, but no one was listening to her and then I saw that Sanne and Adi were standing there talking to the Bulgarian, who I knew sold horse, and then I knew it was over for today, for yesterday, for tonight, and I thought soon I won't be able to cope any more, I'm starting to feel a bit tired, I said to Becca, signalling to her I was going to go and do you want to join me? Riis had excellent images of mortuaries, interiors from sanatoria, children's homes, prisons, mental hospitals and graveyards. He showed an image of three blind beggars and said that he'd managed to accidentally burn down their home because of an incorrectly aimed or incorrectly dosed flash charge at the moment the flash went off (cue laughter from the audience). We cadged fags off people at the central station and then Soot showed me a cubbyhole behind a stairwell I'd never seen before, we sneaked in there, there were a few brats sitting on a bit of cardboard, they were scared of us, but Soot calmed them down with a gesture and a few words I didn't understand, we sat down under a window and rolled a fat one, Soot tagged the wall and I watched, then we passed the last bit to the kids and took off, past a heap of sleeping bags and down into some kind of basement where the lights just went on and on, with walls that were red and then green, and then switched back and forth. As we were walking, Soot said I'd promised we'd go to the sea someday. But how are we going to get there. Riis said: I wanted, with my own eyes, rather than going on the assertions of people who've never seen for themselves, or who've only seen part, to get to the heart of the matter. Furthermore I determined a certain simple measure, with which I set out to assess life in the underworld. Everything intended to foster life and physical and spiritual health was good, and everything that harmed, smothered and restricted life was bad. Becca sat in one of the rooms, she'd worked a double shift and then slept the whole day, now she wanted to cut loose and she was bugging us: let's do something, I've got two days off then I'm working a week straight, I don't give a shit what it is but we've got to do something fun. I dunno, I said sleepily. Let's take the bus, Becca said, or we could borrow a car from someone serious and head out to the coast, have a puff and chill in the sand, swim naked in the sea, it's the shit, jumping off cliffs and that, bring your violin and play for us while we chill in the shade. It'll be fucking cool. I've told you a thousand times it's not a violin. It's a fucking cello and I'm not taking it anywhere. Don't you remember when we lived on the edge of the quarry? That summer we dreamed of *justice for all*, when we sat there smoking on the edge of the cliff, teenagers, *estupidos*, proper junk-heads, and Ponyboy'd knocked out four of his teeth before he turned fifteen and Žana'd had two abortions in a year, it was the record for our part of town, that was the year before she turned sixteen, Ibbe started selling, Zoltan bowed out, turned into a swot but was still hanging out with us, Larsson got us our first pistol, etc., it felt like everything happened that year, the world was ours, you know, the sun hung there like a fucking orange over the water and shone on our skinny little bodies in the evenings, on the cliffs, it was the summer we discovered the Malaysian code of honour (you get three warnings, then I have the right to kill you if I do it with my bare hands) and fell in love with Polish skinhead girls who wore sun crosses, had Celtic crosses tattooed on their cheeks, on their foreheads, on their backs, on their tits, and we told them: you can't be nazis here, you idiots, we're *blattar* here, and we drew lightning bolts and skulls and flowers on our bodies, because we dreamed of *justice for all*, that's what we said, and apparently that included sun crosses on the face and tears in the corner of the eye, a tear for each year in prison, as they said, a tattooed tear for every year, for every friend no longer here, for scars and wounds and hidden fears that multiply and reappear, each day week month so clear, you know the heavy atmosphere, when no one knows who'll overhear and no one dares to be sincere, so close your eyes, forget, close the window, forget, lock the door, forget it all, bed down to sleep, shut down, as they say, make it all disappear, lose yourself in your dream, soon they'll come for you: *yalla* bye! Your time's up, you're the one they're picking up, you're the one on the stretcher, it's your friends crying, they're the ones with new fears, new scars, and you know bro, that's how it goes, as they say, like a real warrior, as they say, and Becca looked at me and I looked at her, and I said of course I remember, of course I remember what they said, all that stuff about freedom and justice, but it was all child's play, it's years before you realise just how damaged you are, how fucked up you got, and you want to tell the kids, you want to warn them, like an older sibling, you want to tell them there's a better life, there are other ways to live, you don't have to be afraid, don't have to defend yourself all the time, but you don't, you don't say anything to them because you know they won't understand what you're saying, not a chance, and even if they did understand they wouldn't take it on board, they just wouldn't, they can't hear it, the same way we didn't hear. You don't realise until years later that the word *free* exists, no, that the *word* free exists, but it has no meaning, I mean, it doesn't denote anything in reality, just like the word *unicorn*, like the word *god*, or I don't know – perhaps it denotes something that isn't in front of me, to the sounds in my headphones that take away part of the world around me, and if I close my eyes everything disappears, and now I can think, I'm not sucking my teeth any more, like Soot, and my tongue is silent and unswollen, unbloodied, I close my eyes and listen, I'm Cody but I don't know it, or perhaps I know but I pretend I don't, I pretend I'm going to live, to grow and become an adult, I hide in a corner of the youth club and listen to this secret music, my secret life, my true life, I pretend it's me playing, I pretend I'm already an adult and that I'm talking, freely and easily, joking and serious, I see myself pointing to the sheet music and discussing something, a glissando or a vibrato, and my arms, my elbows, my wrists, fingers, so light and agile, stable and reliable, I'm a calm person, unafraid, I explain something, I demonstrate something on the cello, my hand in a relaxed grip on the bow, but out of the corner of my eye I see madness encroaching and madness questioning and madness pressing in and pressing down on me, madness threatening to punish me if I don't respond, asking what I'm doing, laughing at the sounds coming from my headphones, I laugh back, stand up, I'm going to get the others and tell them, he says, I turn it off and knee him in the groin, now it's me laughing at him instead, because I see his surprise, he thought I'd back down, and madness sinks down in one body and rises in the other, I kick him in the calves a few times and press my forehead against the bridge of his nose, with small jolts, to push him away. A

pulsating rhythm, a repeating pattern, a regular oscilla-
tion between stronger and weaker points in repeating
cycles of various kinds. Bach's cello suites, where the fuck
did you get that from you little cunt, get out of here, a
sucker punch and a headbutt and there's no one else left
in the room, and my tongue is still silent, unswollen, but
now I know I'm Cody, all this is nothing but waste prod-
ucts and arrested development, toxins that the ruler of
madness is washing from his system, it's an international
dream of beings who can shape-shift, change their appear-
ance, become something else, as though you could go
up to the child, take a good grip on their jaw and say
that in the future, Kyoto clowns will laugh at Romantic
depictions of the primaeval forest, spread hewn-off faces
around themselves and harbour Modernist ballet perfor-
mances inside their frontal lobes, and the angles of their
brow bones will bloom inwards like an infection, so the
lioness can keep the egg warm, incubating the latent
psychoses till they blend with the external, dissociative
ones, with the drugs, that is, which must in turn be dipped
quickly in dopamine, in pools, pools where all this can
be released, pools that reflect all the world's psychoactive
canopies. Fucking monster of a tree that one, says Cody,
roots-vibe discotheque and shit, and then on we go, not
a penny in my pocket or the bank, just two or three gulps
of moonshine in a Coke bottle, one last roofie, man's out
of it now, just one last ball, please, a bout of unipolar
disruption, that's what they said, but we took it easy, bro,
just an old postcard with torn-off corners, a rolled-up
receipt, an empty wrap in our pockets, mementos of
better times. Yeah. It's hopeless, right, as the doctors say
when we can't hear. But we know, we're not stupid, said

Marko when I went to visit him that first week, just cos we have dirty clothes and debts with the authorities it doesn't make us thick in the head, as I said to the pig before he slammed the cell door shut with his vile bastard grin, cop's grin. I swear we've read all those books, Marko went on, with a weird look on his face, what the fuck else are we gonna do with all these years inside, and believe me man, we know everything about all the different leaves and fruits and harvest times and anhedonia and different receptors and shit like the diathesis stress model, have you ever read the Bible, you bastard? I told you: when you're in here the revelations come along like clockwork, one after another, like Chinese firecrackers, like a string of pearls, I told you lot, you shouldn't have given me computer time, paper and a pen, cos when I link my brain up to the internet trippy shit happens, always, you get me, conclusions, analyses and insights come raining down till I'm wading in that shit, so to speak. You know you can request copies of your records? Marko said. Makes for nice reading. The affective syndrome makes it impossible, or at least difficult, to have a functional routine. Over the years, the effects have varied, though certain recurring traits are worth mentioning: feelings of isolation, alienation and inferiority, insomnia, internalisation of the social order. Substance abuse, naturally. It's so thrilling you start making your own notes. I've got to remember to ask the psychologist if we can interpret the alcoholism, with additional short-term substance abuse (cannabis, amphetamines, ketamine, MDMA, benzodiazepines, cocaine (in your dreams, man)), to be a consequence of, or at least to a certain degree linked to, the social phobias that have developed (can I say *blossomed* here?). Other compulsive behaviours. Whose thoughts are you thinking? You're an adult but you see yourself as a damaged child. You see yourself as a victim and therefore feel that your right to this hatred, indiscriminate and to be honest pretty vaguely defined, is unshakeable. You live fully in the shadow of your parents' failures, their losses, their blind struggle. You've got kids to take care of but you go to pieces, breaking down the moment you start thinking about your own childhood. You want to murder the person you see in the mirror, but you daren't, so you swap the mirror for a window. Who's out there? Your self-image leads to a critical situation in which the most important elements are a paralysing fatalism combined with an all-eclipsing defeatism. Shit, bro, said Marko, pausing, all these words. Do you know how it feels to have them in your mouth? Like Tupac said: if we do wanna live a thug life, OK, so stop being cowards and let's have a revolution. But you know what it's like, bro. Only god can judge me. Fatalism, defeatism? Look it up, man, said Marko. It's what's known as *ressentiment* in philosophy, Hakim told me, and Hakim's read more than anyone in this whole place, there's a German guy who's written about it. You should read more philosophy, and Marx, and contemporary political theory, he said, you can find all that shit in books. In the Koran, even in the Bible, trust me. Sure, Tupac's a start, it's good that you're reading his poems and checking out the interviews, it's good, that man got a lot of things right and was well sharp for his age, bearing in mind he was an entertainer, but man, you've got to see the limitations too and step it up, raise it up a level, go above and beyond, you get me brah? Right, bro, course I know that, Marko said to Hakim.

Marko told me all this when I went to visit him. And it was exactly what Soot used to say. I know all about how they come out and photograph us and talk about us in their seminars and conferences. How the other half lives, heroin chic, the proletariat, thug life and spare a little change mate. I say to them: you diligent lab workers, to you human beings in need are just insects you have to stick a pin in so you can study and classify them, you street-level slum Samaritans, you gutter tourists, on the hunt for the next aesthetic wonder, the next imagination-whetting, titillating larva, the next grub who, anticipating metamorphosis, crawls around in the dung covering itself in whatever grot emerges from its orifices, and so on and so forth. I know, said Soot, I know exactly, that's what their artists are like, that's what Soot always said, I've met enough to know, he said, they live off other people, they seek us out, broke monstrosities and oddballs and spectacular freaks, spiritual cripples and that whole undefined, motley, drifting mass who they hand a crust of bread or a handful of coins and then fix with their camera, said Soot, position in front of their easels, their microphone booths, they hound the homeless, the beggars, pissheads, junkies, the criminals, they'd skin a creature alive just cos their still life is crying out for a splash of carmine red, they've got no problem asking the suicide case to throw themselves in front of the train fifty metres further along, so they get the fairground in the background, believe me, that's what they're like, I've seen it for myself, time and again, believe me, bro, I've seen how they pull people's sleeves and beg and ask to be allowed to listen and see and touch the latest hot story, juicy tale, personal, private, honest and raw – but simply and straightforwardly told – portrait of desperation, and in return the teller gets to stroke their soft clothing, to sniff the mimosa and the hyacinth and the lily of the valley they keep in their editors' offices, which those silent cleaners, our mums and dads, have wiped clean with their aching bodies, a pat and a hug, self-congratulation disguised as tenderness and love, believe me, said Soot, and sucked his teeth and spat, I know a thing or two about that stuff, yeah, I know a whole lot of shit about the less tender sides of that tender, nurturing representational apparatus, and Becca said: I believe you bro, I know a few things too about those so-called 'disturbances', but if I say shit about how things are, real talk, and maybe my thoughts about *why* things are the way they are, they look at me with the same expression I imagine a certain person was wearing when he looked at Oliver Twist asking for more food. But it's all right, we know how to take food, right, man, and that's why we laugh at them, right, laugh at them and say: we feel sorry for you, cos we know we're better equipped for the future than you could ever be, with your straight spines and broad smiles, I mean, better equipped for at least *one* future, a possible, potential future where most of what surrounds us now has literally collapsed and been torn apart, caved in on itself, a time where all that remains is struggle; blind, raw struggle for survival. There, weapon in hand, hungry, dirty, plagued by swollen, bloody feet and memories of death and battered comrades, or just the expectation of death and battery, on our side or the enemy's, there, in that place, we'd do better, we say, that's where it would finally become apparent how absurd your world has been up to that point, how bizarre your lives have been, your psyches, even your bodies, the implausibility of all that flabbiness being allowed to exist unthreatened, it would become completely obvious how bizarre these spoilt, secure creatures are, these people, that is, you, who never cast a nervous glance over your shoulders, who never look around before you step into the road, what is that, people who step out of a doorway, a bus, an SUV, *without* looking left, looking right, checking the other side of the street to evaluate the risks, what kind of arrogant, perverted creature treads unfamiliar ground without looking first? Soot looked at her and sort of nodded and shook his head all at once. A creature like that must be a long way from their true nature, Becca went on. Being at ease in that world, I dunno if I can imagine anything more abnormal, anything more ignorant, anything more feeble-minded, and it makes me feel contempt, even when it comes to my sisters, my brothers, my people, my team, the smart ones, the ones who are awake, the ones who've understood the real shit, you know, but they're still naive, running around with this fucking bizarre idea that what they do and think makes any difference at all to the big picture, that they have any part to play in the big game. It's an ease that's just ignorance, stupidity almost, it's the same sort of courage that Alma, my two-year-old niece, has when she tries to jump into the deep end at the pool when she can't swim. They walk out into the road without looking, walk into new rooms without first checking the place out, identifying dangers, threats – for them there *are* no dangers, nothing threatens them. They're comfortable, at home in their bodies, their houses, their neighbourhoods, cities and countries, at home in their lives. Shit, the world is theirs. Feeling at ease in the world, is there anything more twisted, is it even possible to be more conceited? Becca asked Soot, who was now just shaking his head and looking down at his feet, as we walked along in the red-green sheen reflected off the old tiles, as I remember, Soot was dragging his lighter along the wall, making a gentle scraping sound interrupted by the rhythmic click, click, click, click of the joins. For a while it looked like we'd come to some kind of underground traffic crossing with neither traffic nor roads meeting and I heard Soot breathing, his jacket rustled, and I saw Becca pop something into her mouth, a tablet or some chewing gum, and my mouth felt dry but my tongue didn't move, it lay fixed and unswollen under my palate, and I said nothing but thought, shit, I've got all this stuff in my mouth too now man, like a fucking river it's running, even now, when I'm not saying a word. You could hear a pin drop in the hall as Riis turns on the projector. Marey and Muybridge, he says, captured birds in flight and trotting horses with stop-motion photography, and LA Huffman rode alongside his subjects in the territory of Montana and photographed right from the saddle. But the light-sensitivity of the glass plates and the brightness of the optical equipment available didn't yet allow for shooting from the hip or for candid photography in the dark stairwells of the tenements and the dark back alleys. Becca opened a hatch in the ceiling and we clambered out onto the pavement, the evening was dark and cold, an old beggar came up to us and we all shook our heads, and Soot said: I need my change as much as you do, my friend, you can bum a cig but that's all, and Becca said: shit, the old guy's damn shoes must have cost more than mine, and it felt as though someone had started drilling a little hole just behind the bridge of my nose, between my eyes, up into my brain, up into my frontal lobe. Soot and Becca said they were going to head up to her place and you know, take it easy and shit, and so suddenly I was standing there alone in this bright orangey light, seeing my body reflected in the plate glass of the bus stop. Where are all the animals? I thought and saw Cody, half transparent in the plate glass of the bus stop, sweep his gaze across the empty square. The buildings were covered with great dark patches, and these were connected by fracture-like lines that created an irregular, chaotic network above the streets. No animals, said Cody, as though there was anyone there to hear. No animals in sight. He picked up a half-metre-long pipe that was lying on the pavement and went into one of the buildings. An empty, desolate, enormous entrance hall. He wandered around aimlessly for a while, searching for the stairs without finding them. But the lift seemed to work. After a moment's indecision, he entered it and pressed the button for the fourteenth, the uppermost floor. The doors closed and the lift began to rise. Cody observed his face in the mirror, he felt dirty and knew he smelled bad. He listened to his breathing and the distant sound of engines and let the metal pipe slowly glide across his left palm, fingered some debris flaking off one end of it. He wondered where it had come from. Once it had been part of a chair and someone had sat on that chair. Once they'd lived here. Once they'd cycled to the limestone quarry and bathed in the clear water. Once everything was open, uncertain, possible. There'd been a bed there, with freshly washed sheets. A scent, now impossible to recall. Everything in the disengaged face he saw in the mirror had told him he had to jump. Cody had passed the sixth and seventh floors when the lift slowed down. It glided past the eighth, too, before stopping, with a sudden deceleration, on the ninth. The doors opened. Cody was alarmed to see five or six people standing in the dark corridor outside the lift. But he didn't do anything drastic, just took a little step backwards as his grip on the pipe tightened. However, the people took no notice of Cody. There were both men and women, they were light-skinned, had blonde or ash-blonde hair and were smartly dressed. They all had large scars on their faces. Scars that went from ear to ear, as though the corners of their mouths continued, out across their cheeks, out towards their earlobes. On some of them, Cody saw once they'd entered the lift and turned their backs to him, the scars even continued behind their ears and down their necks, towards their spines, where the lines met and, it appeared, continued down their backs. Cody couldn't help imagining how it had looked when these lines were skin sliced open, fresh wounds: he pictured a kind of fishlike creature. Fishlike creatures falling upwards – rising to the surface like bleeding bubbles of life. Then it came to an end. He was driven out. Unable to afford the fee for a hammock or mattress at one of the better hostels, he moved into a police hostel near Church Street. One night in his sleep he was robbed of the gold medallion he always wore on a chain round his neck. Reporting of the theft to the constable on duty – and asserting legal ownership of said object – led to him being thrown out onto the street. Alberta, a stray dog who'd adopted him and had to wait on the street outside the hostel, sank his teeth, in solidarity, into the leg of the policeman who'd thrown him out, at which point the policeman took hold of the dog's hind legs and crushed its skull on the stone steps. His Slavic blood rose and, blind with rage, he went on the rampage, attacking the guard's office with paving stones and assorted cobblestone ammunition. He was soon disarmed by the security guards, escorted to a ferry and conveyed across the river. Behind the abandoned railway lines the vegetation had forced its way through, taking over everything. He saw the sun come up behind the damp birches and rowans, and from a rusty, cracked viaduct, all the pillars of which were richly adorned with wildstyle letters, he saw the beautiful, complex patterns the lines created. Is that Mary Ann Hobbs's voice? he asked Saima, and she nodded and they talked about sounds from *The Breezeblock* and Anti-Gravity Bunny Radio as though it was their world, as though they weren't interlopers or thieves there, and at night he put a sock between the strings and the fingerboard, practising scales and arpeggios while the others were sleeping. Together they could say love in eight languages. Then the plate glass of the bus stop was empty, and I went on alone. It wasn't long before I bumped into this guy Darko, accompanied by a blind donkey he'd christened Yul Brynner, and it turned out he lived near Dalaplan, and because I lived there too – actually no more than a stone's throw, so to speak, from the clinic where we all, a few years later, would be reunited, in a vision, like shadows, in a waking dream, a revelation, with all these speculations going around about our behaviours, our reactions, our needs, desires, our violence, et cetera, as they said, and only another stone's throw from Mobilia, where a few years earlier we'd hung out in gangs, as they put it, stealing and vandalising both private and public property, or buying vodka and fags off the Poles in the car park – I said to Darko I know how to get there, I can help you, we can go together, I'll just finish my drink and then we walked, weaving slightly, through the city with Yul Brynner and Silver Arrow, my bike, this sick mountain bike I'd bought off Maxamed outside the school in Kroksbäck for 500 krona, which was stolen again just a few weeks later, while Bergsgatan was deserted, as it always was at night back then, I was walking with Darko, I was pushing my bike along and he was leading the donkey, the street was deserted and empty, there was fuck all there since The Black Cat had closed, and Darko told me he was from Banja Luka, a crappy little town, he said, and I said just like this one then, and we smoked a fat joint by the statue and spat on the honour of the working man, and he told me he was a double deserter, he'd fled from two different armies, beat that if you can, *brate*, you can't, can you *suedi*, that's what you are after all, that's what he said, and he said he hated refugee centres, where he'd lived before finding a sofa to sleep on near Dalaplan, they were just full of peasants, he said, peasants who beat their wives and children, and I said don't lie *bratku*, you're lying, you're exaggerating, you're the one sounding like a *suedi*, man, and the whole time Yul Brynner was standing there, chewing on something, with a face that said fuck it all, it's like he's hating on us, what's the word, explicitly, no, what's the word, you know, demonstratively you mean, yeah, that's it I guess, and I taught Darko the word ruminate, said Yul Brynner was hating and ruminating, but Darko said donkeys don't ruminate, they don't ruminate or have hooves, he said, which is why you're not meant to eat them, according to Devarim, the Fifth Book of Moses, that is, and I probably looked a little confused when I asked how he knew about that kind of thing, and he told me his grandma was a Serbian Jew from Hungary, that is, from the Kingdoms and Lands represented in the Imperial Council, and the Lands of the Crown of Saint Stephen, as Darko said his grandma used to say, and this grandma had taught him all this, and I said OK, well then we'll give eating the donkey a miss, out of respect for your grandma, god rest her soul, and Darko said he wanted to make a film about Yul Brynner, the real one that is, not the donkey, and it was going to be called *Yul the Sinner*, or maybe *Yul the Winner*, he laughed, pleased with himself, flashing a row of yellow-brown teeth, but I didn't get it, didn't even know who Yul Brynner was, and he told me all about some Bosnian and Yugoslavian authors I'd never heard of either, and he told me an anecdote about this sewage-soaked techno party in Belgrade during the NATO bombings. Nihilism is truth, *brate*, he said, *to je ono pravo*, and then he related this dream he'd had. Just imagine: vultures. On cliffs. Sea and shingle. Sand and drifts of seaweed. The salt water crashing in over the corpses. Black birds leaning forward, pecking and picking and tearing at the flesh, sinewy and heavy. There's a bang. They look up, fly up, unfurl their fantastic wings, fly up even higher, rise, sail away, disappear. In the hand of one of the corpses: a sodden piece of paper, on the paper a compass rose, black and red ink, white background, numbers and letters. It says: *LEO*. I look up and see a sculpture, a lion standing beside a recumbent lioness who's been hit by an arrow, two lion cubs are climbing on her. I walk around the sculpture, and I see that the lion cubs have also each been hit by an arrow. On the back, someone has sprayed *Rex Nihil*, you get it, king of nothing. Trippy, right. I dunno Darko, not sure what to say, it's a bit boring listening to this, to be completely 100 per cent honest with you mate. Then I met him at some illegal club, bloody and totally wasted, he'd jumped up and nutted the ceiling, and I turned round and said Darko, man, you're getting blood all over my shirt, it's like a bad dream, bro, I can't wake up, I take my shirt off, I'm wearing a white vest, we pose and play tough for a French photographer outside the club, a magnificent cul-de-sac, she says, I remember it now, the speed was burning and stinging, Hansson started a fight at the bus stop, everything was frozen like a tongue on a lamp post, one tug and it's all blood and ice and you're hitting yourself in the face again and again, totally shocked, numbed. I wake up. There are voices coming from nowhere. What, *vole*? What do you want? The homes are very simple. Dirt and desperation fill the bare, empty corridors and dangers lurk in every stairwell. Few women venture out after dark. Now Moosmann was playing John Cage's *Souvenir*, gently, restfully, so calmly I began to feel tired and thought I might drift off, but then came a great, heavy, murky cluster of notes, a powerful noise, a sound that both filled my insides and consumed me totally, and something, the movements, the dynamic, held me there, eyes closed but wakeful.

Perhaps there *was* something trembling. Perhaps it was me, perhaps some plant, perhaps something invisible, hidden. Moosmann played *Souvenir* and I opened my eyes and was already on my way, restless, nervous, on the hunt, with the others, on the way to the squat, the bus, all that shit, and I saw us there, relaxing on Becca's worn-out sofa, drinking something, chilling on the balcony, Becca and Kati telling us about the job they'd had in Copenhagen, at a massage salon offering so-called happy endings, they pulled men off for money but they said it wasn't prostitution, it was massage, and the men never, under any circumstances, touched them, and anything but a handy was completely forbidden, any girl who did more got fired on the spot. One time, Becca told us, I tricked Kati, she was new and we pretended to accuse her of having slept with a guy, me and the manager, a dominant sixty-plus madame, she'd been a model in the sixties, I've forgotten her name, she played along and screamed at Kati with this put-on rage, you fucking slag, how could you do this to us, and all this shit, and Kati broke down in the end and we gave her a hug and told her we were only joking, and Becca told us another story too that we taped and sent to a friend, it was a story about how she'd slept with her boyfriend and then afterwards, when he went to the loo, she started masturbating, and he came in and said what are you doing? so she replied I'm having a wank and tasting it and it turned out he didn't know how his sperm tasted and she thought that's the kind of thing you should know and made him taste it and he didn't like it as much as she did, she said, and then they decided to taste their own piss, or she decided, she said, and they each pissed in a glass, they didn't mix, and she tasted hers and he his, he didn't want to but she forced him and that was the whole story, I don't know if you liked it and I don't care either, bye, she said on the recording, and as well as minesweeping myself, I also used to piss in my own beer bottles then put them in strategic places so that the other people minesweeping would get my warm piss in their mouth. I almost died laughing. Later we were sitting on white plastic chairs – so cosmopolitan, someone said, you see them everywhere – drinking Nescafé. You know I hate fucking Nescafé. But you never learned to drink black tea instead? Ah, watch your arse out of here. *You'llneverlearn*, your middle name. Yeah, well I know never to say never. Well I never. Aren't you clever! Top marks. Next stop, university! Naptime, must ring that Daisy or Maisy or whateverhernamewas, fell asleep again on the night bus. Saw the others getting up and going to work. The depiction of the immigrant slums was so hair-raising it was hard to put the book down. In Glasgow it rains constantly. I put my hood up, curl up in a ball and shiver. The whole time I'm scared of being jumped and getting one of those Glasgow smiles, as they call them, having to go around with it forever. You see it now and then in this area around Gorbals.

Skinny, malnourished guys with scars, visible and hidden. But I'm cautious and I train hard. Drive a forklift at a warehouse and really appreciate the camaraderie our team has developed. No racist bullshit, the so-called identitarians keep themselves to themselves and Becca's presence keeps the laddishness at a bearable level, though the gay-haters are another story. I often have visions of getting assaulted, cut, even killed. Sometimes I have visions of doing the assaulting, on the verge of delirium, killing. Hard blows to the larynx. Got stopped by the cops a few weeks back, and the whole time the pig was talking to me, asking his stupid questions he already knew the answers to, the whole time I was imagining beating him shitless. Him begging me to stop, and me going on beating. It made me feel so incredibly calm that in the end the cops said OK, you seem kosher, as they put it, so we'll let you go, but we'll take the gear and next time remember that personal use doesn't mean however much you like, and so on, there are limits, you know, they're flexible, and they're relative with these things, but that doesn't mean they don't exist, and so on, you're on the borderline, you're cool, you have a job, there were no kids about, and so on, we don't think you're selling, but think about this, think about it, kiddo, buddy, laddie, and so on, as per, and I had to do another round, out to the crane, then the gym, then to sleep, then to work, and the whole time I was smashing the cop's larynx in. A quick blow and he's lying down, unable to breathe. Kicks, knees. And so on. One evening I sit in the yard with Aidan M, one of the kids I've got to know here. When his mates aren't here he's not as tense and wired. We laugh at the fact that Aidan's mum called him a sonofabitch, and suddenly his dad comes by and starts talking about the old gangs, telling us about how it goes back a long way in Glasgow, apparently even in the 1700s they were throwing stones at each other down by the Clyde, then the Catholics came over when they were starving in Ireland, and then The Cumbie Boys, Tongs and Toi and Come On were all formed, Die Young and Brighton Billy Boys and Govan Team and all the different Mad Sqwads and Young Teams and whatever else they were called, and now, says Stuart – that's what Aidan's dad was called – every ramshackle fucking tower block, every mouldy little hovel has its own gang protecting the area. But everyone knows, he says with a stupid grin, that it's just about unfucked, bored teenage boys with cheap booze and bad drugs in their veins. Right, Aidan? he says and whacks his son over the back of the head, that's right, you're not dangerous are you, not really, and Aidan pushes Stuart's hand away and says fuck do you know, you fucking cunt, what do you know about me? Come on, his dad says then, I didn't mean anything by it, and Aidan takes off and Stuart shakes his head. He looks at me and laughs for a long time. All mouth, that boy, he says, before bumming two cigs off me and going on his way. Fucking tramp, I think and regret not having Aidan's back. The dreary brick facades that faced onto the street tended, however, to conceal most of the squalor and decay. Passers-by couldn't see much of the slum buildings that grew up in the yards, which were utilised to the last square foot. The ingrained assumption that labourers needed neither sun, air, water nor elbow room proved to be as good as ineradicable. Then Kiko rings and I think I can't take any more, but we're out on the way to a squat somewhere anyway, I'm sitting in a van with

Kiko and Rawna and some guy behind the wheel who I
don't even know and I'm asking where is this place
anyway, and Kiko says Elephant and Castle. For a few
seconds I can't hear or see anything and I'm just thinking
EC, EC, Elephant and Castle, Elephant and Castle. I see
Rawna scratch her left arm, which is covered with some
kind of bleeding rash. And then I remember, the Heygate
Estate, EC, and I say it out loud, there in the car, that that
was where Darek and Amine lived, the guys I worked
with on the *Atropos*, a few years back, and I can suddenly
taste it, feel the nausea in my mouth, as though it was
just yesterday, no, as though it was today, actually, right
here and now. It's about respect and honour and integrity,
all that shit. Standing up for all that they are, even though
they hate all that they are. Everyone knows, deep down
inside, that self-hate is the strongest hate of all. The most
powerful driver. Heygate, Kiko says, doesn't exist any
more. They pulled that shit down, built airy estate agents'
offices or an art gallery or something, Rawna says. Shit,
I'd almost forgotten it, I say to Kiko and Rawna, but now
it's all coming back. So true to life it's actually unpleasant.
As if time has stood still. That taste in my mouth, I say,
a mix of sweat and labour, weed and alcohol, rust and
salt water, the smell of vomit and scopolamine tablets
for the seasickness, it's the taste of Belladonna. I swear,
I say to Kiko and Rawna, Belladonna, what a joke, but
that's what he called her, you know, the captain of the
Atropos, the ship we enrolled on, *Atropos*, the little luxury
cruise ship for bored yuppies with no imagination and
too much money and time. A crappy job, without a doubt,
but still much better than the job I'd had before, behind
the counter in a little porn shop just off the Reeperbahn.

You know, I say to them, at that point I was living on Sternstrasse, on the other side of the fairground, and I used to crawl home in the mornings, past the cop shop and the whores, the piles of crusty punks, crawl over the Heiligengeistfeld, the empty funfair, full of plastic palms and clowns and airbrushed kitsch, overshadowed by this enormous nazi bunker, sunrise and silence, birdsong, fucking depressing, but it still had some kind of draw, that life, that way of dying, protracted, idiotic, low, it suited someone like me, best at being worst, as they say, but yeah, one evening I was sitting drinking in Lehmitz and I started talking to this guy who introduced himself as Mush, we shared a spliff and it turned out he was chief cook on the *Atropos*, and he asked me if I knew my way around an espresso machine, could chop onions, grill a steak and fix a Caesar salad, and I said of course, no problem man, even though I didn't know shit, but he grinned and said the job was mine. Kiko wasn't listening to me any more, he was studying some scrap of paper he'd dug out of his pocket, so I turned to Rawna, who was still scratching away at her scabby arm, and said the *Atropos*, I swear, the first thing you had to learn was which areas were off limits, no-go zones or whatever they were called, and in principle that meant the whole ship, apart from the restaurant itself, the cabins below the waterline, where we slept, and a small area up on deck which was shielded from view so the yuppies wouldn't have to see us any more than necessary. All the people working in the kitchen were men, and all the people working on the floor, that is the waitresses, were women, and behind the bar was a mix. The yuppies were both men and women, mostly white hetero couples, even if the odd black or homo turned up from time to time. We worked Thursday to Tuesday and were off on Wednesdays, when we often took in at some port and picked up new yuppies. The staff was also security guards, glass collectors, a DJ and a so-called restroom valet in a white shirt and black bow tie. Moody, or Moody Blues as some called him, or Moody Black as others called him, or Mulinge as he was actually called, was in the gents; he held out paper towels after the guests had washed their hands and offered them a shower in aftershave: some cheap kind with a chemical citrus scent, an offer they tended to refuse with barely concealed distaste or pity. Mulinge told himself he was there to preserve order, and actually that wasn't completely untrue. Officially it was his job to report any drug abuse, that is, all drug use, to the security guards, whose responsibility it then was to discipline the person who'd committed this illegal act, if necessary with a moderately appropriate degree of violence, as Vinny, the security guard, put it. It goes without saying that no one followed these rules for shit, or we wouldn't have had any guests. In the ladies there was Farai, who didn't have any nickname, perhaps because she never talked to anyone, she never said more than was necessary, never more than *hello, yes, no, I don't know, thank you, please, goodbye.* But Moody insisted that she was extremely smart, studying law via distance learning and that one day she'd be the first female Secretary-General of the United Nations or something like that. Then she won't have to stand in a toilet listening to white people's drunk bullshit any more, then she won't have to work among rich white yuppies farting and pissing, shitting and snorting coke, looking at her with disdain while they dry their hands and blow their noses, apply lipstick or bathe their throats in their own expensive perfume. Maybe then she'd remember her friend Mulinge, who used to stand on the other side of the wall, in an identical room, almost the mirror image, and carry out the same work as her. Maybe then she'll spare a thought for me. I hope so, he said, I hope she doesn't forget her roots, so to speak. We worked together after all, even if we were in separate rooms. I'm stood under the same blinding lights, with the same repulsive noises and the same nauseating smells, I've had the same taste in my mouth after two hours in there. The distinction is I've been among men, and men are a bit different. I guess you know that, everyone does. They're a little more aggressive, a little more dangerous, but I have no problem being in their midst. I command respect. And I'm strong. I can handle most things and most people, he said. And one morning – I was standing there chopping onions, tears in my eyes – I heard Argo ask Moody, who'd come in to collect his wages, why he stayed there, in his *tile-clad kingdom* as he called it, year after year, while the women came and went, as Farai probably would eventually, UN or no UN. He didn't mean anything nasty by it though, right, he just meant Moody was worth much better and so on, but somewhere in there was still the accusation, the question, *why are you debasing yourself?* And I looked out through the hatch and saw Moody rocking his upper body a little as he smiled at Argo. You know . . . Maybe I'm too strong. It's not always good to be strong. You get me? Maybe not, said Argo. Or else you just have to use your strength in the right way. I tipped the chopped onion into our largest pot, swapped knife and chopping board and pulled out a pan of vegetables to be peeled and prepped. But you know, there's some things in life you have no influence over, Moody said. Mario walked past. What are you talking about? Life, man, Moody said. Fate. Fate? I know all about fate, my friend, Mario said. Have you seen my tattoo? I've had it since I was sixteen. He unbuttoned his shirt. In the middle of his chest was written *AMOR FATI*, in heavy capitals, in scar tissue. You have to love your fate, he said laconically. Shit, man, said Argo. Is that a scar? Did it hurt? Mario did his shirt up again. Sometimes pain's a good thing, you know? A reminder, something that heals. You know? Fucking hell, said Argo, love my fate, I don't know to be honest bro. Moody laughed. *Amor fati*, bro. The guy's lost it. Think about it, man, said Mario. This knowledge is older than everything around us. Our forefathers were smarter than us in many ways, and more, how can I put it, in harmony with our nature, if you get me. It's old-school knowledge. Choose your battles. That's what it's about, nothing else. Choose your battles, bro. Suddenly the door was thrown open by Andrea, the alcoholic Italian, who nodded at us and said: Mush here? I shook my head. Go hard, dude. Andrea always played metal at unpleasantly high volumes when he was working. At least when Mush, who liked the kitchen quiet, wasn't there. Later, said Moody, and walked off towards the office as Andrea took out the cassette of trancey techno that Anders, the pill-popping Swedish guy, had been listening to and put on Slipknot's 'People = Shit' at top volume, shrieking *Here we go again, motherfucker* and, with a kind of suppressed rage, pulled out knives, utensils, sacks of onions, pats of butter, bags of flour, sugar and salt, pans of various sizes and chopping boards in various colours, like a bizarre little whizzed-up

cartoon character. Mush was really called Massoud (I don't
know why he was called, or called himself, Mush, my
guess was that some bastard of a chef had called him
Mushroom, and got everyone else to do it too, to keep
the little Arab down). He'd started as a kitchen porter but
had worked his way up, trained himself, and now he was
a chef, chef de cuisine, as he was fond of saying, and he
sat at the bar, drinking cappuccino after cappuccino,
smoking Marlboro Lights and reading recipes, which he
very rarely and almost grudgingly approved of, and if you
went up to him he'd raise a hand as if to say don't disturb
me, and if you didn't go away he'd look at you with a
lopsided smile and say: haven't I told you about my big
balls? Have you ever seen a beetle from behind? I mean
it. I've got big, hairy, extremely heavy balls. Why can't
we see them now, if they're so big, we said. Baggy jeans.
As god is my witness, said Mush. Not particularly baggy,
Mush, we said. Look at Andrea, *that's* baggy. It's an optical
illusion, he said. Andrea's trousers are just full of air. Just
like his head. OK, show us then. What? He smiled. Your
balls, man. Nah, can't do that. Sorry, friends. Only women
get to see them. Men can't handle it, they go crazy with
jealousy. Then they try and kill me. Look. He pointed at
a scar on his neck, seven, eight centimetres long, thick
as an earthworm. And Liz said: just show me then. And
then he turned red and fell silent and held up two fingers
and no one had a clue what that was supposed to mean.
Mush was Algerian and made no secret of the fact he
looked down on the Moroccans, the cook Tahar and the
porter Amine. Tahar was Mush's right-hand man, the sous
chef, as Mush put it, but he was slack and had no cha-
risma. He also suffered from something called bilateral

ptosis, drooping eyelids in both eyes, so it always looked as though he was about to fall asleep, something that brought out his lethargic side even further, and all this probably added up, made Mush feel secure in his position. Amine had low status. He was chef de plonge, chief of the washing-up, or something like that, as Mush said with a grin. He was the one who lived on the Heygate in Elephant and Castle, in a little one-bed flat with his fundamentalist dad. The dad worked as a cleaner on the Tube. They sent money to the rest of the family who lived in some little village in Morocco. Amine was seventeen years old but was still a child in many respects. He was essentially illiterate, was extremely inexperienced and knew very little about the world beyond his dad's flat and the route to and from work. He would come and stand with his face ten centimetres away from yours, and just stand there, breathing and watching what you were doing. It got Anders really riled and he'd hiss: back off, for fuck's sake Amine. Have you never heard of personal space? Personal space? Amine said innocently. Shit. Mush, tell Amine about personal space. No, no, no. You can't. He doesn't get it, it's too complicated. And in Arabic: go down and do the washing-up, Amine. *Yalla emshi*, don't stand here gawping. Fucking peasants. They're like children, Mush might say about the Moroccans, they can't help it. They don't know any better. You have to treat them like that. Like donkeys. Listen, Kiko, I said, are you asleep or what? What's up with you? What's this shit you're staring at? Rawna, listen to me now, this is important, I remember how Andrea used to love winding Amine up too, you know – we used to send the washing-up down to the basement in big blue plastic crates via a little lift, and sometimes he'd come up to check the crates and send them down if they were full, and each time he came into the kitchen, Andrea would force a drink on him. There was a little shelf with white wine, red wine, cognac, rum, pastis and a few other things you might find yourself using while preparing food. Most of it found its way down Andrea's throat, but he was good at hiding it. He knew Amine would get the sack if it came out that he'd been drinking the kitchen booze, we were actually all banned from doing it, but they tended to overlook it with the cooks, and Andrea in particular, since he'd worked there a long time and was good at his job, especially during the lunch rush, when it was most stressful, and before he got smashed. He also knew that drinking alcohol was against Amine's religious convictions. But he still poured a glug or two into a measuring cup and whistled to Amine. Look, for you, my friend. Try it. Amine gave an awkward smile and shook his head nervously. No, no. Not for me. Come on now, Andrea said encouragingly. Be a man. Amine lifted both hands to his face and waved them slowly. Anders walked past with two white five-litre buckets in his hands. Said: let him be, Andrea, with a smile. No, no, no. My father, said Amine and drew his finger across his throat a couple of times. Back and forth. My father will kill me. He stacked the clean dishes on the shelves. How's he going to find out? Andrea laughed, and flung his arms out to the sides. Who's going to tell him? Tahar, would you say anything? Tahar, who was deboning a shoulder of pork, looked at Andrea with tired eyes and just shrugged his shoulders limply. He wasn't particularly amused by Andrea, he never was. Amine put a crate of dirties in the lift and closed the hatch. You Muslims are fucked in the head. Come on Amine. Be a man, screw Tahar, he's just jealous. Amine didn't say anything else, just stood at the sink, washing his hands. OK, be a pussy then. I'll have it, Andrea said, downing the contents. Amine looked away and went down to his station, always the same thing, you know, Mush couldn't really tell the names Andrea and Anders apart, he used to call Andrea Anders and vice versa, or he'd just call them both Andrews, so in the end they both wrote their names in Arabic on the fronts of those white disposable chef's hats we had, so Mush could just shout his *Yalla, yalla!* Work, work! Andesh! Andrah! *Move yourself!* in between the Arabic harangues that had Tahar and Amine clenching their jaws in humiliation, dropping their gazes and going back to mopping the floors, loading up the dishes, scrubbing grease off the stove, or whatever they were doing. Same old, same old, said Rawna, it's the same old shit. It's still raining. What's happening, Kiko? I say. Are we at the Elephant already? Who's driving anyway? Cool it, bro, Rawna says, pulling her sleeve down over her messed-up forearm at last, and I look at her and say nothing at first, but I'm thinking about the mouse on the floor of my room that time she came to see me. Then I can't help myself, and I say Rawna, do you remember? Do you remember that time you stayed with me, when you were trying to come off horse and all that? What are you talking about, she says, leaning her head against the window, which mists up, as if erasing the streets and the rain and the different coloured lights, and I think both of us are thinking about that grotty room in Brixton where she was living with her sister and boyfriend, what was he, Czech or Slovak or something like that, they didn't even have their own bathroom or toilet,

so when you went to visit they had to sit and shoot up
right in front of you, even though they didn't want to,
they just turned round so you didn't see the actual injec-
tion, the actual needle, the actual puncturing, it was a
kind of boundary they'd overstepped and they knew it,
even then. Fuck you talking about, Rawna says again, and
I realise she's embarrassed. That apathetic junkie style is
pretty fucking idiotic if you're not seeing it from the
inside, and if you are it's not long before you're as repel-
lent as any other junkie, from the outside at least, it can
be quite different inside you, and Rawna really had a fire
inside her, she was a lovely person, strong and worldly,
and she was going to get herself out of the worst of it,
not like her sister and that guy she lived with. Rawna
helped me when I was green and my angst got the better
of me, I couldn't cope with that shit, I couldn't switch
off, couldn't sleep, got paranoid, got depressed, and grass
didn't help, and booze only helped a bit, and no one dared
take E on the job. It was like a nightmare, as though the
whole floor was going to swallow me up, down into an
unending hellhole, and I wanted to cry like a child, and
I had to work hard to keep the mask on, and I kept the
mask on, I was hard, but Rawna knew, Rawna saw the
panic, I don't know, in my eyes, in my body language, or
smelled it in my scent, and she just stood beside me and
took my hand, we both stood there like that behind the
bar, it was early evening, not many punters, just a few
yuppies having their post-work beers, we just stood there
side by side in our uniforms, our company shirts, I think
there was a Bacardi logo on the right breast, that cool
logo that was kind of like a bat, and our black aprons,
and in the end I landed, in the future's warm embrace,

with a gentle morning spliff on the top deck of the 38, and she was gentle and freshly fixed up, calm and balanced, with glowing, glistening eyes, and she held my hand, yeah, I was like a child then, it's going to be fine, she said, you'll be fine. So when she said she was going to kick the heroin, of course I was there for her. She came round one afternoon, we hung out, I was drinking and smoking, she was feeling lousy and we sat and chatted, didn't even think about fucking, till I fell asleep on the floor and she lay there writhing and suffering in my bed. I had to work in the morning and she was sleeping when I left, and when I came home that evening there was a dead mouse on the steps, a soft little grey mouse with small pink paws, and Rawna was gone. No note, nothing. And I swear, for a few seconds I thought, kind of against my will, that she was that mouse. That she'd died and that was, like, her real body, that this was quite simply who she was, a little rodent, vermin. You're screwing with me, says Rawna, that never happened, man. You're just screwing around, bro. No way, Rawna, I smile, don't you remember those typewritten messages we used to give each other? *Should I pursue a path so twisted. Should I crawl, defeated and twisted?* And Argo writing: *Why must I be the thief? Why must I be the thief?* Cody, says Rawna, you're talking to someone who's not here. We don't know what you're talking about. I turn to Kiko, but his place in the car is empty. Kiko? Where are you? What do you mean, Rawna? Don't you remember that Montenegrin guy, Marko or Mirko or Mario, yeah, that was it, Mario, who was always chatting about Montenegro's independence from Serbia. Whatever the topic of conversation, whether you were talking about cheese production, holey socks, skunk, turntablism or contemporary Russian literature, anything at all, whatever you were discussing, he could redirect the discussion onto Crna Gora, the Black Mountain, and then he'd sing 'Oj svijetla majska zoro'. *Our future national anthem. Majko naša Crna Goro.* Isn't that important any more? Shit, how come I can remember it then? Kiko? Mario turned to Paola, the Italian girl he called Isabella because he thought, and he was sort of right, that she looked just like a young Isabella Rossellini, but with a gap between her front teeth, and sang 'O sole mio', and said something cheesy, and the bodybuilder David from Madrid offered us some coke, and the bartender Mohammed, he called himself Dan, who tried to hide his hash-smoking during Ramadan – he'd smoke his spliffs in secret in the little staff toilet in the basement, until he realised it was ridiculous, that everyone knew, then he said he'd realised this was between him and god, we could all butt out, though in fact we'd never butted in in the first place, and Darek, the Polish guy who always wanted to hang out with me, who was always washing his clothes in the washing machine, which was only for work clothes, so he wouldn't have to pay for the laundrette, he was constantly sneaking about with some carrier bag full of damp jeans, hoodies and underwear, he was a real bull neck, a real barbarian, a slapstick figure who'd walk into lamp posts while ogling girls with that stupid grin of his, that wide-eyed attitude to queers and their lack of shame, in his face you could see just as much curiosity as panicked fear, I used to shave his head in the filthy staffroom in the basement, between the washing machine and our lockers, the damp concrete and the constant stream of employees coming past to smoke spliffs by the ventilation shaft over the toilet, just like Dan, and what was her name, the Italian girl, not Paola, the other one, the one who was with my dealer, who'd come in to chat shit about the boss, that fucking dickhead, and I'd stand behind Darek who'd be sitting on a crate, watching the washing machine where his clothes were still spinning round and round, and I'd press the clippers against his skull and the whole time he'd say harder, more, deeper, and I pressed that goddamn clipper against his nut with all my strength expecting bits of skin to start flying in every direction any moment, and him just saying harder, *bratku, mocniej*, harder, *mocniej kurwa*, and me pressing and pressing, but he was never satisfied. Fuck Rawna, I should have scalped that little pig, scraped the skin off with Massoud's knives, which he sent off to be sharpened with lasers every other week and when they came back they were so bloody sharp there was always someone cutting themselves and Darek came in and he just wanted to have a look, just have a feel and laugh, *ja pierdolę*, those damn knives are sharp. I shaved my own head with a razor, it was a nice feeling to wake up in the morning a few days after shaving and run your palms with the grain of the hair, to feel that smoothness, and then to draw them backwards, to hear that sandpapery crackle, the roughness, to feel the sleep gradually leave your body. And outside the window of the cabin lay the ocean, the endless sea, the empty, terrifying, meaningless sea, with its rocking and its splashing. The sea, Rawna, do you miss it? Or have you forgotten it? We're sitting in the taxi now, in Glasgow, heading out along the Clyde, on the Southside, out towards Gorbals, where Dima's got something going. Dawid pays for the taxi, he'd already let us have two lines, he's behaving a little strangely, I think, what's with him? Dima laughs hoarsely, he's working in demolition. And lives in a flat that's about to be demolished. Are you going to demolish yourself, mate? Get a wrecking ball and swing it at your head? You know it's true. Now now, don't get your knickers in a twist, says Rawna. Getting dimmer with Dima, he laughs. We go. We had a fair bit of trouble with youth gangs, the old man says, the Mulberry Street Gang, the Cherry Street Gang, and even girl gangs like the notorious Robinettes – in my days it was The Whyos, The Potash, The Molasses Gang and others who threatened Mulberry Street and Five Points. We appointed a special contact and tried to convert the gangs into youth clubs and organisations. There was weightlifting, ball games, fencing, leatherworking, coppersmithing, ceramics, tap and ballet classes and art classes. We got a store of boxing gloves and tried to interest the gangs in resolving their differences with more sporting methods, so to speak. Instead, the club interiors and so on got destroyed a number of times – and on one occasion a pacified gang attempted to raid the organisation's coffers to purchase various weapons for self-defence. Some of the young people's social dysfunction found expression in music, in roughly the same way as in Hell's Kitchen, or Port of Spain, Trinidad – and several calypso bands and a dance orchestra, the Riis Ramblers, achieved a certain degree of fame. I tell them about a job interview in a bookshop James had fixed up. A bookshop in the West End. The Voltaire and Rousseau. A bloody serious bookshop full of old books, with a Czech tea room and everything. Sounds like a normal job, says Dima. Sick. Don't screw it up, bro. It's cushy having normal friends. What do you mean?

Sounds like afternoon tea. What do you think I mean? Seriously, what do you mean? What do you mean, what do I mean? Are you completely thick? He means you've got other, normal friends and we're tramps. Gypsies. Gyppos, for real. That's why it's gonna work out for you. A normal job, a normal life, all that shit. Sounds like a walk in the park on a sunny day. And you? I know, Dima says, pointing at them one by one. Prison, overdose, terrorist, cleaner, social services, loony bin. Ey, how come I'm gonna be a cleaner, that's the worst one. You talk a lot of shit, Dima, I say. You're all gonna be fine. I know it. I'm totally convinced. I'm gonna fuck up this job as per and then everything'll be same old, same old. Same old, same old, says Rawna. Same old, same old. And then? Then? You know. Then. You know what happens then.

The flowers. What was that thing about the flowers? When Moosmann played *Mein Weg hat Gipfel und Wellentäler* there in the cathedral – I could see the fractal structures, how the variations carried us on through the days, one after another, and then yet another, and yet another, year after year, like falling, softly fluted petals, falling, pinkish-white, red and lizard-green, sweet-scented and trembling – I was already sitting on the steps outside, waiting for Argo, crumbling fag butts into a new Rizla, and I heard someone shout: bro! We'd docked at some new nameless port and the others were off to some K-1 gala, but me and Argo wanted to dance so we rang around a bit and got some intel, needed to kill a couple of hours so we headed down to the mega-Tesco, bought some cranberry juice, found a spot in the southern corner of the park and drank our vodka Polski-style, as Darek called it, a slug of booze from the bottle, two slugs of juice from the carton. Argo called me a barbarian. I said that if I was a barbarian I would have been sleeping with him. He said: you can if you want. You sucked that Italian's cock, didn't you? I'll take care of you like no woman ever has. You know that was a mistake, I said. It was more about self-destruction than sexuality, you get me. He grimaced. You'll be the first person I'll call when I come out of the closet, I said. Promise me. I promise. You know, it doesn't mean you're gay. What? If you bang me. It's like in the clink. The one giving isn't affected. Like in Agadir. I've never got as much cock as I did there, but if I'd said to those guys that they were queer they'd have killed me, literally beaten me to death. I was the queer one. They were manly hetero men who were just putting it in a hole, it made no difference whether I was man, woman, animal, black, white, green or meatloaf. You get me? Yeah, I mean, but then I'm a little more sophisticated than that, right. Of course. Fuck, I forgot, you read Mr Whoreman Hesse and you know how to spell fook all. Exactly, except his name is Hermann. Herr Hermann Hesse. OK good. We've got it straight. You're not a barbarian, not gay, not even bi, you're simply a sophisticated hetero. Must be lonely. But maybe you could fuck one of those high horses you love sitting on so much. I laughed. Maybe I will, Argo. As long as they're female, that is. What do they call them? Mare, filly? I'll let you know if it ever goes down, so you can watch. So you can toss off to my thrusting backside. Ooh, so generous, darling. But you know, queens don't sit there staring into horses' cunts. No, they probably don't use the word cunt either. Fuck you. They do sometimes, if they're sufficiently provoked by overstrung hetero-nerds who'd rather sleep with filthy speed-freak slags than shake off their inhibitions. Stop now, I didn't sleep with her and it was a mistake anyway. You know what I've been thinking. Honestly. When we were in that club the first time. All those Muscle Marys, I was actually scared for real. Yeah, they can be really grotesque. Yeah, but I don't mean it that way. I mean I saw how big and strong they were, that they wanted to screw me and I had no way of stopping them. I went to the gents and there were three of them in there, dancing in the piss fumes. It was absurd. Grinding, bare-chested, sweaty, bottle-bronzed packs of muscle. They made me think of those He-Man figures the other boys had when I was little, and they called me cutey and leaned forward over the urinals to look at my floppy dick and made comments so I couldn't piss and it took even longer. And I thought fuck, if they wanted to they could rape me easy as that. Argo laughed. But sweetheart, Muscle Marys can never get it up. All those steroids they stuff themselves with, and the shit they take when they go out. They look hard and they glisten, but inside they're rotten. It's like they've stopped working. But it makes no difference whether they can get it up or not. It's not about that. The interesting thing is that I thought about it, that I experienced something totally new to me, this vulnerability, that their attention was violent in some way. Cody, may I introduce you to your feminine side. Feminine side, here's your ignorant dude side. Well yeah, that's what I thought too, actually. The link between masculinity and that threatening quality, the sexual violence, or whatever you call it. Interesting. Interesting, you think? You weren't scared enough, it seems. What do you mean? You have a lot to learn, man. Shit, I can't be bothered with all this chat, it's too much. It's Friday night, party time. Got to start work soon for fuck's sake. Give the bottle here. We should head to the club soon. Argo burped, took two big gulps from the bottle and grimaced. Later we took a taxi to Anodyne. People were saying that some new genius was going to be playing there with Aril Brikha. In the taxi Argo put his hand on my thigh. I looked at him and laughed. We hugged and he said: you know. If I could have done it in a nice way I probably would have raped you. I patted him on the head. Better grow a few inches taller first, I said. There were a lot of people outside the club, a warm evening light, I immediately felt a joy of some kind burst through me, a warmth in my chest, a pride, a delight, I was alive, I wasn't dead, and as if that wasn't enough, I was enjoying this shitty life. We said hi to a few friends, then dived down into the darkness. Argo paid for me to get in and immediately vanished with some guy, I bought a soft drink, took an E and waited for it to kick in. Suddenly I can smell shit. When I look around I see that a girl who's standing near me is also screwing up her face. Our eyes meet and we start talking about the shit-stink. I start telling her about this basement club in Belgrade. During the NATO bombings they carried on as normal then one night the next building was hit by a bomb, making the sewage in the club overflow. Thousands of litres of shitty water streamed out across the dance floor. We were literally wading in shit, I say. People were puking, and some left, but most stayed there, went on dancing, it was totally magical, totally fucked. Ah, so you were there, she says. Course, I say with a grin. Then she tells me a story about this violent party in the Globe, Shakespeare's theatre in London, a bloody orgy that took place in the 1600s, and she tells me she was there, that she took part in the orgiastic bloodletting, that she remembers it as though it were yesterday. Interesting, I say, tell me more, we laugh and I notice she has a large birthmark on her cheek, far back, right by her ear, I lean forward and I can see it's covered with tiny little strands of hair, the thin, pale fluff you get on brown or black liver spots, what's your name, I ask, and she shakes her head and opens her eyes wide and says: not Eurydice in any case, you tramp, and I regret dropping that E but it's too late, I say as much to her and she shrugs and says it's my loss and we start talking and after a while I start to feel myself gliding away, her voice sounds weird, sped-up, pitched-up, and she says it's a shame, but it's my loss, as she said, and she touches me and the touch is soft and gentle and I say yeah it is a shame, I want to stay there and kiss her, but my body's moving, it's jerking, and I say sorry I have to go now, lean forward and give her a kiss on the cheek, it's even softer and I melt into her and go into a labyrinth wall of singular light and sound, an autonomous space, a distinct time, it's warm and soft there too, but faster, a pulsating, titillating, all-embracing dance, and I try to capture the sound with my body and pour out and dissolve and try to capture the light with my eyes, red and green beams shoot into my head and then there's someone shaking me, are you OK? he asks, better than OK, magnificent, or how should I put it, it felt so good when you put your arm round my shoulder, did you know that, and then a new wave of sound comes, it enters me and I think where are you Argo, where did you go, I miss you now, I want you to embrace me and I send that thought off, something jabs my side but I can drive away the bad feeling, I know how to do it, the guy asks again, far away, are you OK? My eyes roll. For fuck's sake, course I'm OK, what's the problem, it's fine, I say, it's fine, I can take it, and then it continues and it continues, and then they turn on the lights and everything is suddenly ugly with sound that slices into your brain and the thing that raises the hairs on the back of my neck when I know that living

is going to cause me pain for a while now, and I'm thirsty
and I'm trying to find something that can help delay it
but everything is slicing in now, everything's trashy and
filthy, slack, bright, blinding, a guy's begging me for pills,
I'm following someone else around, I don't know them,
we go out into the street, I'm talking to someone else I
don't know about going to some after-party with them,
he looks like someone's trodden on his face, I think,
someone's looking at me in disgust, they call it *nachspiel*,
someone's passing me a line, I don't know what it is but
sniff it up into my skull anyway, ketamine I guess, sniff
it far up, all the way up, as though I've got a special com-
partment for it right in the top of my head, a glowing
bubble of slow light and leaden force, I'm looking for
Argo, feeling like the Pink Panther or that guy with all
the silly walks, everyone's disappearing in front of me,
I'm in a cab with even more people I don't know, counting
my money, just a few coins, the others are talking, I look
at their faces for a long time, thinking that maybe I should
recognise one of them, but no, I don't, and we're getting
out at a metro station I've never seen before, and weirdly
I can't see any sign or anything that says where we are,
we're walking past a buzz stop, I mean a bus stop, where
real people are standing and it feels like they're staring
at me, I'm telling them there's nothing to worry about,
nothing at all, without actually knowing what I mean by
that, then we're going into a narrow stairwell, there are
clothes on the floor, a leather belt which I put round my
neck, as a joke, but I'm thinking of stealing it, then up
two, three flights of stairs, it's like in a film or something,
there are people lying on the floor in a bedroom, there's
music in the room too, gross chill-out that probably fulfils

some function and goes nicely with the nurse porn that's on the TV, I find Budd and Eno's *The Pearl* and put a track on, but this guy starts going crazy, saying it's depressing, that people might start having bad trips and killing themselves, and I'm telling him he's a real fucking imbecile, and if I hadn't been so caned I'd have smashed his nasal bone up into his brain, and I'm wondering where this aggression is coming from and sitting down on the floor, feeling dizzy, mercy, show a little mercy, I'm thinking, and I see a large mortar on the carpet in front of me, looks like marble but I guess it's plastic, but no, this girl is really crushing tablets in it, and sending round a glass plate and a mirror, or a CD, I'm licking the shiny surface and someone's mouth, I can't really see what it is, but it's probably the CD, and in the stairwell they're sucking each other off, I'm thinking about the Italians, the baby in the squat, suddenly feel sick, in several different ways, have to change tack, I go out into the kitchen, sit at the table, stare down into a cleavage, after a while someone slaps my cheek, hello, you OK? she says, course I'm OK, no, better than that, I'm happy, and I'm listening, they're talking about a raid, I'm saying I hate the five-o so fucking much, with all my heart, I say, and I'm talking about my childhood, about how much we hated the five-o when I was a kid, how we'd throw stones at cop cars, how we set fire to a police station, and I spin some tragic story for them, they're captivated, gawping at me, I feel like a bit of a twat but carry on talking anyway, and we're smoking and drinking plain lemon water someone's made, or perhaps there's sugar in it, perhaps it's lemonade, it's good anyway, mind-bogglingly good, I'm sitting there talking, I don't know what I'm talking about any more,

I'm making a case for something, or against something, but three or four people are sitting around me, listening, sending round a spliff, and I'm talking and two of them fall asleep and I'm talking even more and then I'm leaving the kitchen and walking past the guy with the CD and I'm thinking I'm going to nut him but I just grin at him instead, and then I wake up in an armchair cos someone's driven a knife straight into the back of my head, I get up and look out of the window, see a salad and a glass of white wine, it's lunchtime at an open-fronted cafe, I think, and the whiteness of the white shirt astounds or astonishes or assaults me and causes me pain, and I think about how I need to find the toilet now, the pain is tearing my head apart as though a razor blade was running through my brain down into my spine, I get to the bathroom and kneel in front of the toilet and try to vomit up the sharpness but it's stuck, it's stuck fast, I think perhaps this is death, and I almost want to die to escape the pain, it's clear and pure now, like icicles, as though my brain had frozen and was on its way to kill me from the inside with an ice-cold fire and I don't want to live with that, I think, and stick my fingers down my throat, far down, with big, circling motions, as though I was finger-fucking myself in the throat, I think, as though I had a cunt in my face, I think, and despite the unbearableness of everything I want to laugh at that but I can't, and in the end a little liquid comes up but it just hurts my stomach and my throat and my head goes on splitting and pulling me apart, and I think, I can't handle this, I can't handle it, what should I do? I think, what should I do? what should I do? I think a thousand times and I just walk around in a panic, like a pathetic little idiot kid who's lost their parents, everything's unreal, the loneliness is unreal, the pain is unreal, no, hyperreal, the loneliness is hyperreal too, everyone's sleeping, I'm walking around with a knife in my skull, walking around for, I don't know, what feels like hours, but is probably only ten or fifteen minutes, it feels like the whole day and then it lifts, it just runs away, onwards, and I'm absolutely worn out, a little glad I survived, and I lie down in the armchair again, I find a long butt, which I smoke, then fall asleep again, then wake and ring Dima. *Bratku*, wassup? Yeah, yesterday was a lot, but I'm chilling now. Feel like letting loose a bit, man, where are you? The rail yard. On my way. The picturesque groups found in the slum are such that a photographer takes pictures even though his compositional and artistic instincts tell him that the conditions required to take good pictures are, practically speaking, non-existent. The result: a bad image, but not nearly as wretched as the place itself. Wassup Dee, I see you've brought your friends, she says, and looks at me. I stick out a paw. Cody, I say. Belladonna Hex, she says, with a big grin. But *you* can call me Porca Miseria. I hesitate. She laughs. Repeats my name thoughtfully and takes my hand. I look around me. Filthy sofas and yellowy-green walls covered with posters and tags, two crying children, one with a Hitler moustache drawn on, the other with a cock on its forehead and a cunt on its mouth. Just kidding, it's a pleasure, Mr Cody, do they call you Codeine? Hahaha. Sorry, that was bad. She turns to open the safe. Metalheadz logo tattooed on her neck. Her vertebrae stick out. I light a fag and someone gives me a glass of mineral water with something added, says: want some? I down it in one, a weak taste of urine on my tongue afterwards. Argo, Becca, Jakord, Dima.

Everyone was there. Everyone but Mum and Dad, hahaha.
And the prince, of course, gone, what kind of monarchy
is that? What are you up to? *Kurwa*, don't you remember
how it always smelled of cat's piss when you went round
to Olga's place, there was something about the coffee,
something about the acid, ammonia, or whatev – Ah,
Cody? With a C? Yeah. *Come On Die Young*, hahaha! Right?
Isn't it a bit late for that, Becca says. Cody, hahaha! No,
not too late. I reckon you'd draw the line at twenty-seven
or twenty-eight, I think, thirty maybe. What are you,
eighteen, nineteen? Twenty. Twenty, you see, plenty of
time. Hehe. *Come on, die young*, hahaha. You're not quite
with me, right? No not exactly. 'Not exactly' . . . Shit, you're
pretty macho, aren't you, hahaha. Macho man. What?
Me? No. The others chime in. Macho-Smatcho. Ignore her.
Did you know Buffalo Bill was called Cody? Who the fuck's
Buffalo Bill? Biffalo Bull or Bullfight Betty. Aha, you're
ridiculing me, what's the word, getting all delirious up
in my face, to distract me, right, but I can vomit words
too, what the fuck do you want? Something glimmers in
her eyes as she mixes the stuff with a practised hand, her
arms covered in scars and tattoos, burns: yeah yeah. Your
choice, I can play too. Understanding is overrated: when
you leave the shit behind you, you find you've turned to
shit yourself. So mark my words, die young now, man,
die young now, bro, die young now. Come on, die young,
die young now, die now. Cody, what a joke. She gave me
the rucksack. Said: you give it to Slovak, he gives you the
money. It's simple. Don't screw it up. And then she went
out, but she gave me a note: *Come On Die Young*. What's
that supposed to mean? She's just testing you, said Dima.
What are you scared of? I wanted to say to her. But it's

not worth it, cos you can't understand what she's saying. Like it's nonsense, or she's talking in code. It's like you have to have been part of it from the beginning, or have some fucking handbook, a cheat sheet, what do they call it out East, Dima? *Legenda*! Exactly. You need a fucking *legenda*! And Hex came back with a massive grin. Crackers/buddyboo/8er, as we used to say, bitch. You, white, uncircumcised man, please be so good as to show me. Your glans are more sensitive, I've heard, that's why you shoot your loads after three seconds. And can't handle the old grabandbitegames, always choosing the toothless old crones at the whorehouse. Catholic, you say? No shit, you'll have to confess your sins later, I'm a good listener. OK dear, seriously now. Criminal record? Bailiffs? Defaulted debts? Documented drug abuse? Biometrics? That's good, Cody, we should be able to find something for you. We've got a job for everyone, we've got a place for each and every person who needs one. Cody, she mumbled, it can't be fucking true, you know, die young now, my friend, before it's too late. Or actually, do what you want. Makes no difference. Whatever happens, the person you are now is going to die, and die young, either because you stay who you are – in which case this life will kill you – or because you'll become a different person, you'll always be carrying your own corpse within you, you know, like something that lies beneath everything, behind everything, between everything. So now you know, she smiled. OK, you can go now, go and read your Ave Marias. *Pax vobiscum*, or whatever it's called, we'll see what happens, you little *manyook*.

Then everything is still. Night comes and it's impossible to sleep. Day comes and it's impossible to think, to listen. My fingertips have grown soft and sensitive because I haven't played for so long. Someone tries to talk to me, I make an effort, try to focus. This is no home, the voice says, this is just *housing*, Cody. My hands shake. We took long walks in the country to act out our homelessness. We ground our faces into the dirt, crying, held vigils, expressed our sorrow. We lay awake through the night and cried out in abandonment. One Friday afternoon, it's October, autumn, everything's grown colder, I'm standing there waiting for Becca, Dima and the others, they turn up and we head on to this enormous squat that fills a whole apartment building, all five floors. It's fucking full of children, I say to Dawid, who seems to be enjoying it. Fucked-up kids. Really. Full of kids, of teenagers, I mean early teens, bro, actual children, grinning, gum-chewing idiots, but yeah, still decent, four, five floors, a system on every floor, vomit in every room. Yeah yeah, watch the corners. Cold, bare, children passed out against the concrete pillars. What should we do? Ring their mums? Mum's probably collapsed upstairs somewhere, man. And dad's probably out pushing pills in the stairwell. To be fair, the music's good, but I'm not sure I can handle all this shit, I say, but no one hears me. Heavy and dark or fast and euphoric or just straight-up banging music on distorted speakers, ripped-off electricity, no heating, you could see your breath, wall of sound, noise, drums, bass, drums and walls of harmonies and disharmonies. Two steps this way, two steps that. Pirate radio, pirate mates. And everyone doing deals. With wires hanging from the ceiling and wires strewn on the ground, toilets no more than holes in the ground, you piss and shit down into them, wiping yourself with whatever you can find. Or not at all. You spoilt bourgeois cunt. Who said that? I'm ashamed. See myself as though from the outside: see Becca kissing Cody and pushing half an E into his mouth. See the kids in big puffa jackets selling whatever and see, on the narrow, claustrophobic stairs, a woman with a newborn in a sling. A guy's written *fok u* on his forehead and he lights a little glass pipe, it bubbles and gurgles and someone laughs in a reedy voice behind them. Dima flicks away a cigarette butt aggressively. Oh fucking hell, a baby, here. We walk on, pushy dealers in my face with their eyes and their baggies, their puffa jackets and bling. I look around me. Is she really standing there with her goddamn kid? I stop, but this isn't the right moment, they're pulling at me. Don't talk to them, for fuck's sake, we've got what we came here for. The bloodshot whites and smoke smoke, plastic plastic, a fag, a spliff, a bag of pills, a bag of powder, wraps and straws, yellow stripes and red stripes, white lines, blue stamps, pink stamps, Playboy bunnies, Mercedes logos, scraps of paper, Rizlas, folded notes, wads of notes, note clips, glittering and glinting, fuckin chancers, we start to dance, grey floor, light it up, man, *Light It Up* motherfucker – light it up, grey floor black air, black light. Go ahead pass it – go ahead pass it. Grey floor black floor, heavy air. Light that shit – pass that shit. We start dancing, but grey floor heavy air mind racing. Oh, oh, oh, Becca grins all mashed. Nothing's happening, someone moans. Can't get high enough, Dima mouths. Ah shit, please, let me out, I don't think I can handle that smoke-wreathed newborn right now. And that filthy junkie whore of a mother. Proper ho. Filth. I say to Dawid I swear bro, I'm gonna freak if I don't get out of here. What's up, Dawid says, don't you like this place? It's sick. Yeah. No, I can't hack it, I say. What is it, whitey? Cosy Cody, my sweet little blue-eyed pearl of a virgin prince, feeling a little threatened or what? Dawid says. I just can't hack it, I say. We're not kids any more. I'm getting aggressive. It's gonna end with me bashing someone's head in. Fuck you. You get so fuckin moralistic and bourgeois and coplike as soon as children are involved, how the fuck do you know that some Suzuki-and-Montessori brat has a better deal than that little tyke. What the fuck do you know bout that chick, Dawid says. Fuck you man, I say. Everyone in the group was disappointed that the tallest hill in the area was wreathed in cloud, but when the sun suddenly came out and the hill emerged from behind the clouds, tears came to his eyes and he started dashing around like a little kid, shrieking with joy: 'God did that for me! God wanted me to see his creation!' I go down, and out, and I leave them, leave the whole building, quickly, breathing out, hearing the music, a cacophony, a mixture of the sounds from each floor, I can still hear it, must be a whole kilometre away, empty industrial units, viaducts, fences, grates, invisible dogs

barking, bizarre rhythms when the wind snatches the
sounds, the sounds of three or four dance floors, barking,
somewhere a freight train clattering, I pause and exhale
now, no longer racing, walk home the whole, long way
through the night, it's raining, I've been warned, I'm
walking, it's a dark night, an empty residential area
now, lights in a few windows on the fifth, seventh, ninth
floors, but no traffic, yellow light, a burnt-yellow glow,
dark-blue sky, black bushes, buildings, my steps scraping
rhythmically, keys jangling, I'm almost dancing out the
bass on the first and third beats, the bass drum, drum
roll, rimshot, and my steps, yeah, the coins or the keys
in my pocket, yeah, boom shaka tick click boom shaka
tick, boom shaka tick click boom shaka tick, my shoes,
the soles of my shoes, my pulse races when I see a shadow
cross my path, tell myself nothing usually happens. How
many times have you wandered home like this, I think,
and nothing's ever happened, or at least nothing you
couldn't talk yourself out of, or run away from, or if the
worst comes to the worst, fight yourself out of. Little
things have happened, but nothing serious and actually
nothing that hasn't happened in daylight. I don't carry a
knife, I don't carry a knife any more, it's a bit like being
a child again, afraid of the dark, that feeling in your
stomach, that strong impulse, turn round, run, hide, you
won't make it, you can't take it, but I carry on, defy my
body, ignore the impulses, walk into the subway, remember how Tanya used to call these subways rape tunnels,
and I walk where the light is strong, colder, more green
and blue, and I see beginners' tags, like my brother's
when we tried to teach him, my brother, when he got
paint on his face and was pissed cos he couldn't bend the

lines like he wanted to, my brother's narrow wrists and
the spray can's fsssssst, and its fsst fsst fsst, and run as
fast as you can, *bratku*. My brother, where is he now, why
didn't I help him, why did I betray him, forgive me,
brother, I'm sorry, and the light is still strong in the
subway, yeah, more green and blue, and on the ground
there's some trash, and I lean against the wall, against
the lines, the stains, and I light a fag I'd saved and then
I'm out again, into the thick darkness, hearing the distant
roar of the motorway and thinking just carry on carry on
carry on, yeah, carry on walking, I like it, is that weird,
I like being scared, is that weird, or maybe I just like it
afterwards, when you're out the other side, nothing
happened, it's a bit of adrenaline, that's all, you're on
your own, it's dark, all the shit that happens, you know
it happens, it happens all over the place, the whole time,
but not here, that's how you have to think, not now, not
behind this dark building, in this subway, no muggers,
no nazis, but it's on you if anything happens, they've
warned you, don't walk home alone at night, you'll be
mugged murdered beaten to death raped, don't do it,
don't do it, but I've always done it, walked on my own,
walked home alone at night, when everyone else had
gone back to theirs, when everything was done, I pretended I was going home too, but instead I'd swing by
some shop and buy beer or wine or vodka and sit on the
steps in the corner of the park, it was so quiet and the
darkness in the park was so compact, I smoked the last
of the hash and leaned my back against the rough brick
wall and I felt something, it was something big, I felt I
was going to live a little longer, a few years longer, that
I wasn't dead, not yet, and I felt happy. Perhaps I didn't

deserve it, but I was happy. And of course I saw that everything was out of sync. False and wrong. And unsustainable. And that I would and should be punished for it in some way or other, in the end, that was clear, of course, but the feeling didn't stick, it slipped away, I stamped it down, walked on and laughed at everything, and then I immediately felt I should be punished for that too, but that didn't stick either, because I felt the grace, felt it come coursing towards and through me, from above, from below, I don't know, but I felt something coursing. Sure, my punishment was coming, but wouldn't be handed down yet, now was a time of grace, now I was sitting here on these stone steps in the darkness and my body was filled with extraordinary force, with life, and I sat quietly and took the cigarette and held it against my forearm and held it against the thin skin on the inside of my forearm and held it there as long as I could until I couldn't any more and I drank the last dregs and stubbed the cigarette out and went home and at home there was a little vodka left in a glass on the kitchen table and I downed it and put the radio on, turned the dial to the night show, the calm one, heard a choir and lay down on the kitchen floor, and I caught sight of the knives on their magnetic strip and I got up and took the two largest ones, one in each hand, and lay on the floor again and lay on my back for a while, felt the energy and the calm and the silence and that I would go on living a little longer, a little while longer, perhaps a few years longer, everything was good, it was fine, my body could really hold all this, my body stretched out from the deep flow of dark silt under me, which was also my body, chill caves with moisture-covered stalagmites and stalactites, paths and tracks forking off, and more paths, narrower and narrower, further and further into the Earth's crust, which was also my body, it stretched out from this underground territory up to the surface and the chest and head that met the world and the legs and arms and knives, on the points of which everything was gathered, in a concentrated form, on the tiny surface that could puncture, could be stuck into a body, and I lay like that, and felt a fantastically heavy rocking motion, and I felt my body was alive and that it would live a while longer, and then I fell into a slumber, happily, in some way astonished that everything could be so simple, so pure and uncomplicated, just then, at night, when everything else was shut off, when everyone else was fast asleep, when everything was resting, just a few stealthy creatures of the night moving in the darkness, and here and there the watchful eye of the law, but on the whole calm and quiet, and I climbed up on the viaduct where Soot had once practised his wildstyle, over the fence on the south side to avoid having to go round to the big steps, taking care not to tear my jacket, and I got into the rail yard on the other side, jumped down by the postal-service loading bays, saw that one of the doors was open and that two figures were sitting there, smoking, I raised an arm and nodded a greeting but they didn't reply, just looked at me suspiciously, then I spat on the ground, felt the hunger coming and walked on to the bus station, looking at the times and at the clock and thinking about everything that was happening in that precise moment, right now, precisely right now, and then I counted the coins in my pocket, went and bought a cup of tea, dropped in seven sugar cubes without the old dear behind the counter noticing, sat on the pavement and closed my eyes and drank and thought about Dima and the others and that *now* I'm thinking about them and *now* it's already happened, and that *now* I'm living, but it will be over soon, and that *now* we're living and *now* someone's dying, and I think again that someone's dying *now*, right *now*, that it's happening again, and again, and again, in loads of different places, in loads of different ways, in completely different ways, with different implications, and I think about how we say rest in peace, and I think about how the person who dies actually is left in peace, really released, about how that's how it is, it really must be that way, that when you've died no one can disturb you any longer, so why all that grief when someone leaves us, why aren't we happy for them? Why are we incapable of feeling glad about things that happen outside our field of vision, things that happen when we look away, things that are happening in one place when we're living in another place? And just as I'm thinking about all that, when I've stood up and begun to walk, when I'm thinking about death and funerals and peace and all that, about joy, fields of vision, perspective, about the impact of place on everything, on our whole way of thinking, about our whole way of seeing, our whole way of hearing, tasting, feeling, all of it, when I'm thinking I have to head home, to lie down, that I'm so tired now, I just want to sleep, I just want to lie down and fall asleep, rest my body, rest my mind, just then I hear a voice, someone saying: ey, bro. And I turn round, and he's walking like three, four metres behind me, walking quickly towards me. White top and big shiny watch. Ey, wanna score? Gak, speed, skunk, E, horse? I laugh to myself a little, no, that's enough, I think, that's enough for today. I'm so tired. No, I'm all right thanks, I smile, it's cool, and now he's walking up to me, close, and saying: buy my stuff, you're gonna buy my stuff, and his face is really close to mine and I know something's off. Buy my stuff, he repeats. *Spoko, bratku*, I say, still smiling. Chill. And I tell him I don't have any money, at the same time as I know it's wrong to say that. What does it have to do with him? Then comes the first blow, to my face, and I'm surprised, not sure what's happening. Then comes the kick to my ribs and a few more punches, not particularly hard, but the ones that hit my face seem to smoulder on, burning, with a pulsating heat, in an almost pleasant, enjoyable way, in spite of the concern and fear growing in my stomach and chest, and somewhere in my brain something falls into place and I catch sight of him, he looks blind, with empty holes where his eyes should be, and the whole time he's repeating *buy it, you're gonna buy it*, and the spinning subsides, everything slows down, I come to my senses somewhat, the fear becomes a wave of rage, I regain my balance, focus my gaze, steady myself and go at him, punching, I don't know how many blows, three, maybe four, and I get hold of his hair, knee-ing him in the face, we fall down and I continue to hit him, suddenly realise he's completely limp and has stopped resisting, I get up, he lies unmoving, head kind of angled weirdly against the traffic island, and I look around, someone's walking towards me, I turn my back on them and walk away, or half run, over to the train station, the waiting room, sneak into the toilet and rinse off the blood, drinking water from the tap, my hands are shaking and I'm feeling kind of sick, I try to calm myself down, walk over to the big departures board, check the

time and platform number, sit down and wait, looking
up at the strip lights I can kind of see them flickering like
extremely fast strobes and I think I'm probably the only
one who can see this right now. Everyone else can just
see a single stream of light, a constant glow, but I can see
it sputtering, see it flickering, I can see the pauses and it
stings and aches, my cheekbone, my chest, my knuckles,
my temples. Are the cops going to come now? What
actually happened? I look up at the TV showing black-
and-white images of marionettes. Well yeah, it's true,
says an elderly woman, in the community centres we
played badminton, chess, bowling and so on. There was
this one gang where all the members had a criminal past,
they started getting into marionette theatre. Called themselves The Riis Puppeteers. They performed at all these
charity galas and on the radio too. When the shaking has
calmed down a little I light a cigarette, and when the
train comes I step aboard. I'm feeling really terrible now,
I think. Houses, windows, streets, trees, everything rushes
past. I get off and wander around. I'm feeling terrible and
I walk around for a long time. I don't really know where
I should go or what I should do. The cigarette runs out
and I start looking for butts by the entrance to a shopping
centre. It feels like people are staring at me and I put my
hood up. I smoke butts and try to figure out what I should
do next, but I can't, because every time I think a thought,
a thousand other thoughts flood in and I can't distinguish
between them. I know I have to sleep but I don't know
where and it hurts way too much, I won't be able to fall
asleep without taking something and I don't have anything and I don't have any money. I'm just kind of walking
round and round or back and forth by the canal, near the

hostel, think that maybe I'll run into someone who can sell me something on tab, so I can sleep and then sort everything out later, but it doesn't seem I'll be able to pull that off, and I'm on the verge of tears, I sit down on a bench and cry for a few seconds before quickly pulling myself together, realising that my chest hurts way too much for me to ignore and that I have to get to a hospital or at least a doctor. I get up from the bench and walk on. After a while I pass a guy smoking near the canal bridge, not far from the police station, and I turn towards him as I pass and ask if he can spare any change for the homeless. He looks at me coolly as he digs around in his pocket and hands me twenty krona. He hands it to me with a quiet *here you are* and I take it off him and stick it in the pocket of my jacket. I want to ask him for a cigarette too but the words kind of stick in my chest, and I feel it aching, and the strain in my face. He's smoking, looking at me, as though he's waiting for me to do something, either walk away or say something, ask for something more, and I don't know why, but I just stand there, looking at his hands, at the lit cigarette and the smoke, and our gazes meet, and I get the sense he's stable in some way, that I can trust him, and then I hear myself say: I don't know where I'm going to sleep and I got beaten up yesterday. He squints a little and looks at the cut on my face. Who beat you up? he says. I try to reply, try to explain, but all that comes out is indecipherable mumbling. I want to explain but I can't. I just shake my head and spit on the ground. I have to . . . I begin, but the rest disappears and I grimace a bit from the pain, which shoots through me. I'm thirsty and he says: brah, you should probably find a doctor's or something. I laugh, he doesn't look like the type who says brah much, and the pain shoots through me again. Shit, I say, I was just walking along thinking the same thing, get me. Yeah, sounds good, he says. It doesn't look too good. Have a good one, man, I say. He waves. Take care of yourself, bro. I turn my back on him and leave. Fuck you, *bro*, I think. The pain just keeps getting more and more intense, I think I have to get to a hospital, have to make up some story about where I've been and what's happened so the police don't get involved. Now at least I have money for the bus, I think, and turn the corner to walk over to the central station where the bus stops are. I walk past a girl who I bum a cigarette off and then sit on some steps and smoke it. I nod off and stand up to stop myself falling asleep there on the ground. A little way off a bike is leaning unlocked against a utility box. I can't see anyone nearby, so I take it quickly, jump up on the saddle and I'm a little way out into the junction before I catch sight of the bus that's coming towards me much too fast. *Bro*, I think.

Dear readers,

As well as relying on bookshop sales, And Other Stories relies on sub-scriptions from people like you for many of our books, whose stories other publishers often consider too risky to take on.

Our subscribers don't just make the books physically happen. They also help us approach booksellers, because we can demonstrate that our books already have readers and fans. And they give us the security to publish in line with our values, which are collaborative, imaginative and 'shamelessly literary'.

All of our subscribers:

- receive a first-edition copy of each of the books they subscribe to
- are thanked by name at the end of our subscriber-supported books
- receive little extras from us by way of thank you, for example: postcards created by our authors

BECOME A SUBSCRIBER,
OR GIVE A SUBSCRIPTION TO A FRIEND

Visit andotherstories.org/subscriptions to help make our books happen. You can subscribe to books we're in the process of making. To purchase books we have already published, we urge you to support your local or favourite bookshop and order directly from them – the often unsung heroes of publishing.

OTHER WAYS TO GET INVOLVED

If you'd like to know about upcoming events and reading groups (our foreign-language reading groups help us choose books to publish, for example) you can:

- join our mailing list at: andotherstories.org
- follow us on Twitter: @andothertweets
- join us on Facebook: facebook.com/AndOtherStoriesBooks
- admire our books on Instagram: @andotherpics
- follow our blog: andotherstories.org/ampersand

This book was made possible thanks to the support of:

Aaron McEnery
Aaron Schneider
Abigail Charlesworth
Abigail Walton
Adam Lenson
Adrian Astur Alvarez
Adriana Lopez
Ailsa Peate
Aisha McLean
Aisling Reina
Ajay Sharma
Alan McMonagle
Alan Simpson
Alastair Gillespie
Alessandra Lupski
  Raja
Alex Fleming
Alex Hoffman
Alex Liebman
Alex Lockwood
Alex Pearce
Alex Ramsey
Alexander Bunin
Alexander Barbour
Alexandra Citron
Alexandra de Verseg-
  Roesch
Alexandra Stewart
Alexandra Stewart
Alfred Birnbaum
Ali Conway
Ali Riley
Ali Smith
Alicia Bishop
Alison Hardy
Alison Lock
Alison Winston
Aliya Rashid
Alyse Ceirante
Alyssa Rinaldi
Alyssa Tauber
Amado Floresca
Amalia Gladhart

Amanda Silvester
Amanda
Amanda Greenstein
Amanda Read
Amelia Ashton
Amelia Dowe
Amine Hamadache
Amitav Hajra
Amy Arnold
Amy Benson
Amy Bojang
Amy Savage
Andrea Barlien
Andrea Reece
Andrew Kerr-Jarrett
Andrew Lees
Andrew Marston
Andrew McCallum
Andrew Rego
Andy Marshall
Andy Turner
Aneesa Higgins
Angela Everitt
Angus Walker
Ann Menzies
Anna Corbett
Anna Finneran
Anna Glendenning
Anna Milsom
Anna Zaranko
Anne Alderton
Anne Carus
Anne Craven
Anne Guest
Anne Higgins
Anne Ryden
Anne Sticksel
Anne Willborn
Anne-Marie Renshaw
Anneliese O'Malley
Annie McDermott
Anonymous
Anthea Morton

Anthony Brown
Anthony Cotton
Anthony Quinn
Antoni Centofanti
Antonia Lloyd-Jones
Antonia Saske
Antony Pearce
Aoife Boyd
Archie Davies
Asako Serizawa
Audrey Mash
Audrey Small
Aviv Teller
Barbara Mellor
Barbara Robinson
Barbara Wheatley
Barbara Spicer
Barry John Fletcher
Bart Van Overmeire
Ben Schofield
Ben Thornton
Ben Walter
Benjamin Judge
Bettina Rogerson
Beverly Jackson
Bianca Duec
Bianca Jackson
Bianca Winter
Bill Fletcher
Bjørnar Djupevik
  Hagen
Bobbi Collins
Brendan Monroe
Briallen Hopper
Brian Anderson
Brian Byrne
Brian Callaghan
Bridget Gill
Brigita Ptackova
Bronx River Books
Caitlin Halpern
Callie Steven
Cameron Lindo

Camilla Imperiali
Carla Carpenter
Carla Castanos
Carolina Pineiro
Caroline Lodge
Caroline Smith
Caroline West
Cassidy Hughes
Catharine
    Braithwaite
Catherine Blanchard
Catherine Lambert
Catherine Tolo
Catherine Williamson
Catie Kosinski
Catriona Gibbs
Cecilia Rossi
Cecilia Uribe
Chantal Wright
Charlene Huggins
Charles Dee Mitchell
Charles Fernyhough
Charles Raby
Charlie Cook
Charlie Errock
Charlotte Briggs
Charlotte Coulthard
Charlotte Holtam
Charlotte Ryland
Charlotte Whittle
China Miéville
Chris Gostick
Chris Gribble
Chris Maguire
Chris Stevenson
Chris & Kathleen
    Repper-Day
Christian Schuhmann
Christine Hudnall
Christine and Nigel
    Wycherley
Christopher Allen
Christopher Homfray
Christopher Mitchell
Christopher Stout

Christopher Young
Ciara Ní Riain
Claire Adams
Claire Brooksby
Claire Williams
Clarice Borges
Cliona Quigley
Clive Bellingham
Cody Copeland
Colin Denyer
Colin Matthews
Colin Hewlett
Collin Brooke
Connie Muttock
Courtney Lilly
Cyrus Massoudi
Daisy Savage
Dale Wisely
Dan Parkinson
Daniel Arnold
Daniel Coxon
Daniel Gillespie
Daniel Hahn
Daniel Jàrmai
Daniel Ng
Daniel Pope
Daniel Raper
Daniel Stewart
Daniel Venn
Daniel Wood
Daniela Steierberg
Danny Millum
Darcy Hurford
Darina Brejtrova
Dave Lander
David Anderson
David Ball
David Bevan
David Gould
David Hebblethwaite
David Higgins
David Johnson-Davies
David Kinnaird
David F Long
David McIntyre

David Miller
David Musgrave
David Richardson
David Shriver
David Smith
David Steege
Dean Taucher
Debbie Ballin
Debbie McKee
Debbie Pinfold
Declan Gardner
Declan O'Driscoll
Deirdre Nic Mhathuna
Delaina Haslam
Denis Larose
Denton Djurasevich
Derek Taylor-
    Vrsalovich
Diana Digges
Diana Hutchison
Diane Humphries
Dinesh Prasad
Dominic Nolan
Dominick Santa
    Cattarina
Dominique Brocard
Dorothy Bottrell
Duncan Clubb
Duncan Macgregor
Duncan Marks
Dyanne Prinsen
Earl James
Ed Burness
Ed Tronick
Ekaterina Beliakova
Eleanor Maier
Elif Aganoglu
Elina Zicmane
Elisabeth Cook
Elizabeth Braswell
Elizabeth Dillon
Elizabeth Draper
Elizabeth Franz
Elizabeth Guss
Elizabeth Leach

Jacqueline Haskell
Jacqueline Lademann
Jacqueline Ting Lin
Jacqueline Vint
Jacqui Jackson
James Attlee
James Beck
James Crossley
James Cubbon
James Dahm
James Lehmann
James Lesniak
James Portlock
James Russell
James Scudamore
Jamie Cox
Jamie Walsh
Jane Anderton
Jane Dolman
Jane Fairweather
Jane Roberts
Jane Roberts
Jane Woollard
Janne Støen
Jannik Lyhne
Jasmine Gideon
Jasmine Haniff
Jayne Watson
JC Sutcliffe
Jeanne Guyon
Jeannie Lambert
Jeff Collins
Jeff Questad
Jeff Van Campen
Jeffrey Danielson
Jen Calleja
Jenifer Logie
Jennifer Arnold
Jennifer Bernstein
Jennifer Humbert
Jennifer Robare
Jennifer Watts
Jennifer Wiegele
Jennifer Obrien
Jenny Huth

Jenny Newton
Jeremy Koenig
Jess Howard-Armitage
Jesse Coleman
Jessica Kibler
Jessica Laine
Jessica Martin
Jessica Queree
Jethro Soutar
Jo Goodall
Jo Harding
Joanna Luloff
Joanne Alder
Joanne Osborn
Joanne Smith
Joao Pedro Bragatti
   Winckler
JoDee Brandon
Jodie Adams
Joe Bratccher
Joe Huggins
Joel Swerdlow
Joelle Young
Johanna Eliasson
Johannes Georg Zipp
John Bennett
John Berube
John Bogg
John Conway
John Down
John Gent
John Higginson
John Hodgson
John Kelly
John Mckee
John Royley
John Shaw
John Steigerwald
John Winkelman
John Wyatt
Jon Riches
Jonathan Blaney
Jonathan Fiedler
Jonathan Huston
Jonathan Watkiss

Jonny Kiehlmann
Jorge Cino
Jorid Martinsen
Joseph Hiller
Joseph Schreiber
Josh Calvo
Josh Sumner
Joshua Davis
Joshua McNamara
Joy Paul
Judith Austin
Judith Gruet-Kaye
Julia Harkey D'Angelo
Julia Rochester
Julia Sutton-Mattocks
Julie Greenwalt
Julie Winter
Juliet and Nick Davies
Juliet Swann
Justin Ahlbach
Justine Sherwood
Kaarina Hollo
Karen Waloschek
Karen Woodhead
Kasper Haakansson
Kasper Hartmann
Kat Burdon
Kate Attwooll
Kate Beswick
Kate Gardner
Kate Shires
Katharina Liehr
Katharine Freeman
Katherine Mackinnon
Katharine Robbins
Katherine Sotejeff-
   Wilson
Kathryn Dawson
Kathryn Edwards
Kathryn Oliver
Kathryn Williams
Katie Brown
Katie Grant
Katie Lewin
Katie Wolstencroft

Katie Smart
Katy West
Keila Vall
Keith Walker
Kenneth Blythe
Kenneth Michaels
Kent McKernan
Kerry Parke
Kieran Rollin
Kieron James
Kim McGowan
Kirsten Hey
Kirsten Murchison
Kirsten Ward
Kirsty Doole
KL Ee
Kris Ann Trimis
Kristin Djuve
Krystine Phelps
Lana Selby
Lara Vergnaud
Laura Blasena
Laura Williams
Lauren Carroll
Lauren Rea
Laurence Laluyaux
Laurie Sheck & Jim
    Peck
Leanne Radojkovich
Lee Harbour
Liliana Lobato
Lillie Rosen
Lily Hersov
Lindsay Brammer
Lindsey Ford
Lindsey Stuart
Line Langebek
    Knudsen
Linette Arthurton
    Bruno
Lisa Agostini
Lisa Leahigh
Lisa Simpson
Liz Clifford
Liz Ketch

Liz Wilding
Lola Boorman
Lorna Bleach
Lorna Scott Fox
Lottie Smith
Louise Evans
Louise Greebverg
Louise Smith
Luc Daley
Luc Verstraete
Lucia Rotheray
Lucy Beevor
Lucy Gorman
Lucy Moffatt
Luke Healey
Luke Loftiss
Lydia Trethewey
Lyn Curthoys
Lynn Fung
Lynn Martin
M Manfre
Madeleine Kleinwort
Mads Pihl
    Rasmussen
Maeve Lambe
Maggie Kerkman
Maggie Livesey
Mahan L Ellison &
    K Ashley Dickson
Malgorzata Rokicka
Marcel Schlamowitz
Margaret Jull Costa
Margaret Cushen
Margo Gorman
Maria Ahnhem Farrar
Maria Hill
Maria Lomunno
Maria Pia Tissot
Mariana Bode
Marie Cloutier
Marie Donnelly
Marike Dokter
Marina Castledine
Mario Sifuentez
Marja S Laaksonen

Mark Harris
Mark Huband
Mark Sargent
Mark Sheets
Mark Sztyber
Mark Waters
Marlene Adkins
Martha Nicholson
Martin Brown
Martin Munro
Martin Price
Mary Brockson
Mary Byrne
Mary Heiss
Mary Nash
Mary Wang
Mary Ellen Nagle
Mathieu Trudeau
Matt Davies
Matt Greene
Matt Jones
Matt O'Connor
Matthew Adamson
Matthew Armstrong
Matthew Banash
Matthew Cullinan
Matthew Eatough
Matthew Francis
Matthew Gill
Matthew Hiscock
Matthew Lowe
Matthew Rhymer
Matthew Warshauer
Matthew Woodman
Matty Ross
Maurice Mengel
Max Cairnduff
Max Garrone
Max Longman
Meaghan Delahunt
Meg Lovelock
Megan Oxholm
Megan Wittling
Melanie Tebb
Melissa Beck

Melissa da Silveira
  Serpa
Melissa Quignon-
  Finch
Melynda Nuss
Meredith Jones
Michael Aguilar
Michael Bichko
Michael Carver
Michael Coutts
Michael Gavin
Michael Kuhn
Michael Moran
Michael Roess
Michael
  Schneiderman
Michael Shayer
Michael Ward
Michael James
  Eastwood
Michelle Lotherington
Milla Rautio
Miriam McBride
Moira Sweeney
Molly Foster
Mona Arshi
Moray Teale
Morgan Lyons
MP Boardman
Muireann Maguire
Myles Nolan
N Tsolak
Nan Craig
Nancy Jacobson
Nancy Oakes
Naomi Kruger
Natalie Charles
Natalie & Richard
Nathalie Atkinson
Nathan Rowley
Nathan Weida
Neferti Tadiar
Nicholas Brown
Nick Chapman
Nick Flegel

Nick James
Nick Nelson
  & Rachel Eley
Nick Rombes
Nick Sidwell
Nick Twemlow
Nicola Hart
Nicola Mira
Nicola Sandiford
Nicola Todd
Nicole Matteini
Nigel Fishburn
Nina Alexandersen
Nina de la Mer
Nora Hart
Odilia Corneth
Olga Zilberbourg
Olivia Payne
Olivia Turner
Pamela Ritchie
Pamela Tao
Pat Bevins
Patricia Appleyard
Patricia Aronsson
Paul Cray
Paul Daintry
Paul Jones
Paul Munday
Paul Myatt
Paul Robinson
Paul Scott
Paul Segal
Paula Edwards
Paula Ely
Pauline Westerbarkey
Pavlos Stavropoulos
Penelope Hewett
  Brown
Peter Griffin
Peter McBain
Peter McCambridge
Peter Rowland
Peter Wells
Petra Stapp
Philip Lewis

Philip Lom
Philip Nulty
Philip Scott
Philip Warren
Philipp Jarke
Phoebe Harrison
Pia Figge
Piet Van Bockstal
Pippa Tolfts
Polly Morris
PRAH Foundation
Rachael de Moravia
Rachael Williams
Rachel Andrews
Rachel Carter
Rachel Darnley-Smith
Rachel Goodall
Rachel Matheson
Rachel Van Riel
Rachel Watkins
Ralph Cowling
Rebecca Braun
Rebecca Carter
Rebecca Fearnley
Rebecca Gaskell
Rebecca Moss
Rebecca Peer
Rebecca Rosenthal
Rebekka Bremmer
Rhiannon Armstrong
Rich Sutherland
Richard Ashcroft
Richard Bauer
Richard Carter
Richard Mansell
Richard Priest
Richard Shea
Richard Soundy
Richard Santos
Richard Steward
Rishi Dastidar
Rita O'Brien
Robert Gillett
Robert Hamilton
Robert Hannah

Robin Taylor
Roger Newton
Roger Ramsden
Rory Williamson
Rosalind May
Rosalind Ramsay
Rosie Pinhorn
Ross Trenzinger
Rowan Sullivan
Roxanne O'Del Ablett
Roz Simpson
Ruby Kane
Rupert Ziziros
Ruth Morgan
Ruth Porter
Sabine Griffiths
Sabine Little
Sally Baker
Sally Foreman
Sally Hall
Sally Whitehill
Sam Gordon
Sam Reese
Sam Stern
Samantha Cox
Samantha Walton
Samuel Crosby
Sara Sherwood
Sara Quiroz
Sarah Arboleda
Sarah Booker
Sarah Elizabeth
Sarah Forster
Sarah Lucas
Sarah Pybus
Sarah Roff
Scott Astrada
Scott Chiddister
Sean Birnie
Sean McDonagh
Sean McGivern
Shane Horgan
Shannon Knapp
Sharon Dogar
Sharon Mccammon

Shauna Gilligan
Sheila Packa
Sheryl Jermyn
Shira Lob
Sian Hannah
Simon James
Simon Pitney
Simon Robertson
Simonette Foletti
Siriol Hugh-Jones
SK Grout
Sonia McLintock
Sophie Morris
Sophia Wickham
ST Dabbagh
Stacy Rodgers
Stefanie Schrank
Stefano Mula
Stephan Eggum
Stephanie Lacava
Stephanie Smee
Stephen Pearsall
Steve Dearden
Steven Willborn
Stu Sherman
Stuart Wilkinson
Sunny Payson
Susan Bates
Susan Howard
Susan Winter
Susie Sell
Suzanne Kirkham
Sylvie Zannier-Betts
Tamara Larsen
Tania Hershman
Tara Roman
Tasmin Maitland
Teresa Werner
Thom Keep
Thomas Mitchell
Thomas van den Bout
Tiffany Lehr
Tim Kelly
Tim Scott
Tim Theroux

Timothy Pilbrow
Tina Andrews
Tina Rotherham-
  Winqvist
Toby Halsey
Toby Hyam
Toby Ryan
Todd Greenwood
Tom Darby
Tom Doyle
Tom Franklin
Tom Gray
Tom Stafford
Tom Whatmore
Tony Bastow
Tory Jeffay
Tracey Martin
Tracy Heuring
Tracy Northup
Trevor Wald
Val Challen
Valerie O'Riordan
Valerie Sirr
Vanessa Heggie
Vanessa Nolan
Veronica Barnsley
Vicky van der Luit
Victor Meadowcroft
Victoria Edgar
Victoria Goodbody
Victoria Huggins
Victoria Maitland
Victoria Steeves
Vijay Pattisapu
Vikki O'Neill
Walter Fircowycz
Walter Smedley
Wendy Langridge
William Dennehy
William Franklin
William Mackenzie
Yasmin Alam
Yoora Yi Tenen
Zachary Hope
Zoë Brasier

ANDRZEJ TICHÝ was born in Prague to a Polish mother and a Czech father. He has lived in Sweden since 1981. The author of five novels, two short-story collections and a wide range of non-fiction and criticism, Tichý is widely recognised as one of the most important novelists of his generation. *Wretchedness* (*Eländet*) was shortlisted for the 2016 August Prize and won the 2018 Eyvind Johnson Prize.

A translator and lover of Swedish and Norwegian literature, NICHOLA SMALLEY is also publicist at And Other Stories and an escaped academic – in 2014 she finished her PhD at UCL exploring the use of contemporary urban vernaculars in Swedish and UK rap and literature. Her translations range from *Jogo Bonito* by Henrik Brandão Jönsson (Yellow Jersey Press), a Swedish book about Brazilian football, to the latest novel by Norwegian superstar Jostein Gaarder, *An Unreliable Man* (Weidenfeld & Nicolson).